ID 40

D-40

THE TREASURE
OF ST. WOODY

Other books in this series:

The Flying Wagon
Miss Dempsey's School for Gunslingers
Finest Frontier Town in the West
The Legend of Shamus McGinty's Gold

THE TREASURE
OF ST. WOODY

•

I. J. Parnham

AVALON BOOKS
NEW YORK

Published by Thomas Bouregy & Co., Inc.
160 Madison Avenue, New York, NY 10016

Library of Congress Cataloging-in-Publication Data

Parnham, I. J.
    The treasure of St. Woody / I.J. Parnham.
        p. cm.
    ISBN 978-0-8034-9971-3
    I. Title.

PS3616.A763T74 2009
813'.6—dc22

                            2009003691

PRINTED IN THE UNITED STATES OF AMERICA
ON ACID-FREE PAPER
BY HADDON CRAFTSMEN, BLOOMSBURG, PENNSYLVANIA

Chapter One

*F*ergal O'Brien's raised hand made Randolph McDougal pull back on the reins, drawing their wagon to a halt atop a small rise. With their clear and honest eyes the two brave tonic sellers considered the frontier town of Fort Arlen, nestling in a hollow in the far distance.

"We're finally here," Randolph said, turning to Fergal. "I can't believe that today we might finally discover the truth about the treasure of Saint Woody."

"We could, but where should we begin our quest?"

"I'd suggest we find the fearless lawman Marshal Colt T Blood. If that man can't help us, then perhaps nobody can."

"That's a good plan, Randolph." Fergal sighed wistfully. *"Provided we don't encounter any suffering people before we find him."*

"I know. Then we must put the needs of those requiring help before our own needs."

"So many wrongs," Fergal murmured, *"so little time, and just the two of us to make them all right."*

—Extract from an untitled novel by
Harlan Finchley

"Will it work?" Christopher Tate asked.

Fergal O'Brien shook the bottle, making the amber tonic sparkle in the pale morning sunlight.

"It sure will. This tonic cures anything and everything. It's a universal remedy. No injury is so bad, no ailment is so painful, no condition is so embarrassing that this amber liquid cannot cure."

"How much?"

"The universal remedy can be yours for just a dollar."

Christopher rubbed his chin, pondering, then turned on his heel and headed back into his house.

"Just wait there," he called over his shoulder. "I'll show you the patient."

Fergal rubbed his hands with barely suppressed glee while his partner Randolph McDougal rocked from foot to foot in irritation at this delay. Their traveling show had been ten miles out of Fort Arlen when they'd met Christopher. The farmer had told them a hard-luck story about an illness in the family, and as Fergal never could pass up an opportunity to sell another bottle of his tonic they'd taken a detour to his dugout.

Christopher emerged from his house with the patient tucked under an arm. The sick individual was two feet long, pink, squealing, and had a curly tail.

"It's a pig," Fergal murmured.

"Sure is," Christopher said, holding out the squawking piglet. "And he's mighty sick. Can your tonic cure him?"

Fergal spread his arms in a benevolent gesture.

"I am confident it will be as successful on this little one as it has been on all my two-legged patients."

Christopher sighed with relief, having failed to notice the flaw in Fergal's declaration.

"In that case, I'll buy five bottles." He rummaged in his pocket and withdrew a handful of coins, which rapidly disappeared into Fergal's pocket. "Most of my other pigs aren't well either. Come in and see what you can do."

Christopher turned to go back into his house. Fergal moved to follow him, but Randolph grabbed his arm.

"Fergal," he urged in a low but insistent voice, "look at that man. He keeps his animals with him in a dugout in the ground. He can't afford to pay five dollars for a tonic that won't do nothing but make his pigs even sicker."

"You don't know that for sure. It might work on them." Fergal waggled a reproachful finger at Randolph then winked. "And besides, if it doesn't, he'll know what he's having for dinner tonight."

Randolph released his grip and let Fergal follow Christopher. With a sorry shake of the head he sat on the back of their wagon and listened to Fergal bustle around inside the house, interspersed with frequent squeals, each sounding more aggrieved than the last. After one particularly loud shriek, Christopher emerged.

"I can't bear to watch them get their medicine," he said, cringing. "How long do you reckon it'll take to work?"

"I'm sure they'll be fine soon enough," Randolph said, trying to put as much assurance into his voice as possible.

"You heading on to Fort Arlen afterwards?"

"Sure." Randolph jumped down from the wagon. "We have our show of authentic historical memorabilia to present."

Christopher looked past Randolph into the wagon to consider their exhibits then reached in to withdraw the nearest item, a sheaf of papers.

"And what's this one?" he asked, tapping a finger against the topmost sheet.

"That's one of our most intriguing and educational exhibits—the original manuscript of a Mark Twain novel."

"The adventures of Tim Sawyer," Christopher said, reading the title. "I knew he'd written a book about someone called Tom. Is this one about his brother?"

Randolph coughed. "No. This is the original manuscript of the Tom Sawyer novel, with all of Mark Twain's original spelling mistakes intact."

"A fascinating insight indeed," Christopher murmured.

"And here's another one," Randolph said, speaking quickly to avoid Christopher thinking too much about the suspect manuscript. He took the papers from him then drew his attention to a large casket. "This here is our prize exhibit—the treasure of Saint Woody."

"There's a saint called Woody?"

"There sure is, and in this here casket is his treasure."

Christopher appraised the casket. It was closed, six feet long, three feet high and three feet wide. Solid bands of rusting iron covered each edge and the lid was rounded. Set around a thin slot and projecting out of the lid by a half-inch were five jeweled circles. Each circle contained twelve jewels and around each jewel there were stylized carvings of animals and people.

"And what is that treasure?" Christopher asked.

"Some say it's the keys to heaven itself." Randolph sighed. If Fergal were here instead of inside the house inflicting his tonic to cure all ills on Christopher's pigs he'd relate the full story Fergal had dreamed up to entice people into parting with their money. But the squealing emerging from inside worried Randolph into being honest. "We just don't know. We've had the casket for six months, but we can't open it no matter what we do. So we're on a quest to find whoever built it, Saint Woody himself. We'd heard he lives in Fort Arlen."

"A saint lives in Fort Arlen? That has to be wrong. The only famous person who's ever lived around these parts is Marshal Colt T Blood, and he's not real." Christopher furrowed his brow, then smiled. "But now that I think about it . . . *Saint* Woody. Yeah, I do know him. You'll find him at the fort."

Randolph had long ago accepted they'd never be so lucky as to actually find the man who had created their prize exhibit, but as Christopher had cheered him with this revelation, he smiled then patted the lid.

"That's good news. So would you like to try to get in the casket yourself? We usually charge a dollar but you can try for free."

"What do I do?"

"Turn the circles on the lid to a new position then insert a coin in the slot in the middle." Randolph pointed at the slot then handed Christopher a penny. "If you find the right combination, we've been told it'll open the casket and you'll get to win the treasure of Saint Woody."

"Whatever that might be," Christopher said, twirling the circles until they formed a new configuration. Then he inserted the coin in the slot, which landed inside with a dull thud.

With a grinding of gears, the jeweled circles turned, each one revolving in the opposite direction to the circle beside it as, inside the casket, the penny rattled back and forth, taking a complex route. Finally, the coin rattled to a halt and, with a fateful clunk, the circles stopped moving, coming to rest in a different position to what they had been in before.

But the casket remained closed.

"You didn't win the treasure," Randolph said, offering a sympathetic smile. "What that is will have to remain a mystery, at least until we get to meet this Saint Woody."

As yet another loud shriek from inside the house rent the air, Christopher looked over to the door then back at the casket.

"Knowing Saint Woody, it's my guess that there is no treasure in the casket, after all, just the money people put in it trying to win the treasure in the first place."

Randolph bit his bottom lip to suppress a wince as Christopher instantly worked out what other people usually took a while to decide for themselves.

"You are a most perceptive man, but we're still convinced there really is treasure inside, and maybe even the keys to heaven itself."

"Perhaps, but I'm not—" A clink sounded. Then the penny emerged from a hole in the bottom of the casket, rolled along the end of the wagon and fell off to land at Randolph's feet.

Randolph lunged forward to trap the coin beneath his right boot.

"Now that was a surprise," he said, offering an abashed smile.

Christopher glared down at Randolph's foot.

"That casket's not got no money nor no treasure in it," he muttered, his face reddening. "It's just a cheap huckster's trick. People put coins in that slot, thinking they'll win heaps of money if they find the combination that opens the casket, but you've bored a hole in it so all their money falls out the bottom for you to collect."

"Possibly," Randolph murmured as Christopher correctly deduced how he and Fergal earned a living from displaying a casket they couldn't open.

Christopher raised his eyes from looking at the trapped penny to look at the original manuscript of *The Adventures of Tim Sawyer.* Then he roved his gaze over their other exhibits: Lieutenant Colonel George Custer's personal report on the battle of the Little Big Horn, Santa Anna's wooden leg, unfortunately the right one . . .

As from inside the house another squeal sounded, the penny finally dropped, and not just the one that had fallen out of the box.

"You're both cheap hucksters," Christopher declared. "Your treasure of Saint Woody is a huckster's trick, your authentic historical exhibits are all things you've made yourself, badly, and that tonic to cure all ills your partner's feeding my pigs isn't going to work."

Randolph opened his mouth to refute the allegation but at that moment a particularly aggrieved shriek sounded. Then Fergal hurtled out of the house, closely followed by several hundredweight of enraged hog.

"Run," Fergal shouted. "Pig stampede!"

Chapter Two

"*L*et me go," the unfortunate man pleaded. He strained against his bonds but he found that his two captors had chained him to the railroad tracks securely and he couldn't move his limbs. His spread arms were chained to one track, his bound legs to the other.

"We sure would like to oblige," Rick Hunter said, looming over him.

"But only," his errant brother Garth said, "after you've given us a name and a place."

The man looked up at his captors but he found no comfort there.

A patch covered Rick's left eye, an angry scar cut a jagged path across his broken nose. Two gunbelts crossed Garth's barrel-like chest.

As if to impress upon him the urgency of the situation the mournful whistle from an approaching train sounded.

"So you just want to know what's happened to your missing brother Frank and then you'll let me go?" the man asked.

Rick smirked as he withdrew a key from his pocket.

"Yup. Talk and I'll unlock those chains before the train makes everyone call you shorty."

"I don't know what happened to him," the man spluttered, his voice high-pitched with fear, "but the man you need to see is Marshal Colt T Blood. You'll find him in Fort Arlen."

Rick nodded, judging that this information sounded plausible. The train was heading to Fort Arlen and the fearless lawman Marshal Blood did reside there.

"You just bought yourself our gratitude," Rick said.

Rick glanced at the train, now emitting an insistent scream as the engineer locked the wheels in a doomed attempt to avoid the obstruction on the tracks. The engine was four hundred yards away and would reach them in around thirty seconds. He shrugged then turned away.

"Hey," the man shouted. "What about me?"

Rick turned back and appraised the man's predicament with a cruel gleam in his eye. He mockingly dangled the key between two out-stretched fingers, licking his lips as he waited for the train to get even closer.

The man's cries grew more desperate as the train thundered on, its brakes sparking against the wheels, its whistle screeching so desperately it almost sounded as if it was in pain.

Then, at the last possible moment, Rick threw the key to Garth.

Garth missed it.

"Whoops," he said.

"Next stop Fort Arlen," the conductor said, making his way down the aisle.

Harlan Finchley squirmed with anticipation and shuffled forward until he was sitting on the edge of his seat.

While watching the plains drift by, he tried to suppress the smile that had threatened to break out for the last two hours then gave up the losing battle and let himself grin. But when the person sitting facing him gave him a bemused glare he took deep breaths to calm himself down so that he didn't appear quite so disconcertingly happy.

When that attempt failed and a smile broke out again, he tried to distract himself by reading the Marshal Blood dime novel he'd bought along to pass the time, *The Lost City of Gold.*

Harlan read a few lines, but even Marshal Blood's

latest adventure couldn't hold his attention, not when he was near to completing his journey.

He looked over the seats at the rest of the car and the man who had just come on to the train drew his attention. This man was struggling to maneuver a bulging carpetbag down the aisle.

Harlan stared at him, as he had done when any new person had come on to the train because to him, this far west, everyone was fascinating. But when the man sat and cast a quick glance around the car, Harlan looked out the window to avoid being caught staring.

He pressed his cheek to the cool window, eager to catch his first sight of Fort Arlen, even though it was unlikely he'd see it for at least another hour.

On his journey he'd already enjoyed seeing cowboys board the train and had even seen men openly wearing six-shooters, but Fort Arlen would be a far more exciting experience. According to the Marshal Blood dime novels, Fort Arlen was where the marshal plied his trade, bringing an endless stream of surly bandits and gun-toting outlaws to justice.

Harlan was pleased he wasn't as young as he had been when he'd first read about Marshal Blood. Then he'd believed Blood to be a real person. Now he knew he was a fictional creation.

But his adventures were so detailed and so authentic, he must have been based on a real person and the adventures he had in Fort Arlen had to be based on real events.

So in his desire to write his own dime novel, he needed to see first-hand the rip-roaring action he'd read about, and the best place for him to do that was in Fort Arlen, the scene of so many—

A sudden thought hit Harlan.

Now that he was thinking back to those adventures he recalled how Marshal Blood had caught his first outlaw. A man had come onto a train with a dozen rifles loaded into a bulging carpetbag. He'd handed out the rifles to accomplices already on the train and they'd embarked on a plan to raid the passengers, until Blood had stepped in.

Harlan considered the newcomer to the train, deciding he looked shifty and suspicious. Harlan didn't have a gun and neither did he have the courage to do what Blood had done to foil the raid, but he did have another option. So he stood and drew the conductor's attention, then explained his theory to the increasingly incredulous looking man.

"And how do you know that carpetbag is full of rifles?" the conductor asked.

Harlan tucked his Marshal Blood book into his pocket and shrugged.

"I'm just observant, I guess."

The conductor blew out his cheeks while looking at the man with the bag, debating whether to act. Then with a resigned grunt that suggested he thought events would turn out badly no matter what he did, he trudged down the aisle with Harlan trailing in his wake.

"What's in the bag?" the conductor asked when he reached the man's seat.

The man flinched, darting his gaze around the car in a furtive manner that confirmed to Harlan that he had to be guilty.

"Sticks," he said.

"You expect me to believe that?" The conductor reached down and opened the bag to reveal a heap of sticks, as promised. He rummaged through the top layers, but revealed only more sticks.

"Hey," the man whined, barging the conductor aside, but this had the unfortunate result of toppling the bag over and spilling the sticks over the floor.

"But . . ." Harlan murmured, staring down at the exposed contents. "Why would anyone—?"

The conductor grabbed his arm and pushed him towards his seat, then bent to help the man gather up his property.

Embarrassed now, Harlan made his hurried way back to his seat with his cheeks burning. Luckily, nobody paid him much attention as they were too busy enjoying the entertaining spectacle of two men hunting down the spilled sticks that were rolling around the car.

As his first foray into getting involved in an adventure had gone so badly, he decided it would be a good time to immerse himself in Marshal Blood's latest tale.

He made himself comfortable and crossed his

fingers while hoping he'd find some real adventure soon and not just a man with a bag full of sticks, then began reading about real life in the action-packed West.

Marshal Ed Buckley sighed with joy as he reached the end of the page.

"That Marshal Blood sure is some lawman," he said to himself.

He turned over the page, but before he could find out if Blood would be able to bring the latest bandit gang that had ridden into town to justice, Sergeant Emerson Dodge hurried into the law office.

"You've got to come quickly, Marshal. We've got trouble."

"Trouble?" Buckley murmured, unenthusiastically expecting the worst. In a quiet town like Fort Arlen, trouble usually meant someone had tripped over the boardwalk or a wheel had fallen off a wagon.

"Yeah, and this time it's real trouble. You're not too busy for that, are you?"

Buckley hurriedly dropped the book on his desk.

"I'm never too busy for real trouble." He rummaged in the bottom drawer for his six-shooter, blew the dust off it, then followed Emerson outside. "Have some real outlaws ridden into town?"

"Nope. I've found a useful lead on one of your current investigations down at the fort."

"But I haven't got any . . ."

Buckley sighed. He did have one wanted poster outside the law office, but the possibility of a new lead on the ongoing spate of pig rustling didn't fill him with enthusiasm.

With all of his initial interest having faded away, Buckley plodded after Emerson to the fort, which as usual had wide-open gates. Only one guard was on duty and he was sitting back against the corner post with his hat pulled down over his eyes enjoying his afternoon siesta, even though it was still late morning.

They headed inside and looked around. The square was unoccupied, as usual, aside from several horses lazily appraising them from the stables and a pile of boots and uniforms sitting beside a washtub waiting for someone to gather up enough enthusiasm to wash them.

"So," Buckley said, "where's the lead that'll help me catch the pig rustler?"

"It was here." Emerson looked over towards the mess hall.

Buckley followed his gaze and saw several troopers looking through the window at them. In a sleepy fort like Fort Arlen it was unusual for anyone to be awake this early in the day. They were also laughing and pointing.

Buckley had started to turn when he heard thundering hooves. Then Emerson shrieked and jumped aside as a huge hog barreled across the square, heading straight for them. Its small eyes were wild and it was bellowing like a runaway train as it drove onwards.

Both men dived to the ground, letting the hog pass between them before it pounded on across the yard and disappeared into the armory.

"So the lead is a runaway hog?" Buckley said, picking himself up.

Emerson shrugged. "A wild hog on the loose might be connected to your pig rustler."

Buckley admitted this could be the case with an unenthusiastic nod. Then he swung round to face the armory, wondering what Marshal Blood would do in this situation.

He decided that Blood had never had the misfortune to waste his time on trivial matters such as rounding up a maverick hog, but that didn't change his duty. So he rolled his shoulders and strode towards the armory door.

"So, you ugly varmint," he said through gritted teeth, putting on what he fondly imagined was a Marshal Blood accent as he settled his stance before the door, "either we can settle this the easy way, or the hard way."

Chapter Three

*R*ick Hunter and his brother Garth swaggered into the Lucky Star, Fort Arlen's largest saloon. The piano player stopped playing and when the customers looked up and saw them, a collective gulp tore apart the silence.

"See what the gentlemen want," the bartender said to the saloon girl, Sally.

She fluffed her hair and sashayed towards them, but when Rick spat on the floor and eyed her with steady malevolence, she gulped and scurried behind the bar to hide.

As usual, Old Walt was littering up one end of the bar, but to clear a space Garth kicked his legs from under him. Walt's frail form landed heavily. On the floor he took one look at Garth's yellow

19

teeth bared in a rabid grin, then whimpered and scampered outside.

"Whiskey," *Rick muttered, slamming a fist on the bar.*

"In a dirty glass," *Garth added.*

As the bartender poured their drinks with a shaking hand, Rick looked around until his arrogant gaze alighted on the man who stood at the other end of the bar, the fearless lawman Marshal Colt T Blood.

With an arrogant gleam in his beady right eye, Rick Hunter paced down the bar. He looked Marshal Blood up and down then spat on his boots, but in response the lawman merely hunched over his whiskey and smiled at Sally, who was cowering behind the bar.

"Don't you go worrying yourself, ma'am," *he whispered, his usual soft and comforting voice making her sigh with relief.*

But his calm mood did nothing to soothe the enraged Rick, who grabbed his shoulder then swung him round.

"Marshal Blood," *he muttered threateningly,* "I don't like you drinking in my saloon."

For long moments the lawman considered Rick with his steely gaze, then tipped his hat.

"Then, I'll leave."

"Hey, I still don't like your attitude." *Rick fingered his gunbelt.* "So if you ever think about *drinking in here again, remember this—I'm the meanest shot in Kansas."*

A smile flickered across Marshal Blood's craggy face as he sauntered by Rick, his footfalls echoing in the otherwise silent room. When he reached the swinging doors he stopped and turned.

"And you need to remember this," he said through gritted teeth, his former placid mood gone as he settled his stance, "I'm not from Kansas. So, you ugly varmint, we can either settle this the easy way, or the hard way."

Harlan Finchley put down his book and looked around the Lazy Sow Saloon.

For the last hour he'd been nursing a coffee while reading the last chapters of *The Lost City of Gold.* He'd seen nothing interesting happen yet but he continued to survey the customers, waiting for the excitement to start.

So far Fort Arlen had been a disappointment to him.

The fort dominated the town and through the open gateway he'd seen only a few troopers lounging around. The rest of the town was equally peaceful, but Harlan had read enough dime novels to know the apparent quietness would be shattered soon, and quite probably in the next few minutes.

At the table beside him a poker game was approaching a showdown and that had to lead to trouble.

"I've beaten you," one player shouted, slapping his cards down on the table.

"You haven't," the man sitting opposite him said, sneering as he eyed the cards. "You cheated."

Harlan drew out his pen and paper then swung round to face the table so he wouldn't miss what happened next. In the Marshal Blood adventures, cheating at the poker table always led to one result.

"If you reckon I cheated," the accused player said, rolling his shoulders, "what are you going to do about it?"

For long moments the two men considered each other across the table until the accuser tipped back his hat.

"I reckon I'll demand my fifty cents back or I won't buy the next round of drinks."

This statement of intent received a chorus of grunted support from the other players, and so with a rueful smile the cheating player pushed the pot across the table.

"Take the money, then." He uttered a defiant laugh. "But I reckon that means I'll just need to be a bit sneakier the next time to fool your eagle eyes."

Everyone laughed. As the dealer collected the cards for the next hand and everyone ragged the cheating player about his poor attempt at cheating, Harlan muttered to himself with disappointment then dropped the paper on the table.

The poker games he'd read about were always high stakes, someone always got accused of cheating, and gunplay was the only way to settle the dispute. But these men were playing for cents and they thought it amusing that one of them had tried to cheat.

He was still casting aggrieved glances at the players when a new and more promising source of trouble walked into the saloon. The trail-dirty newcomer stood a pace in from the swinging doors and slowly looked around the room with narrowed eyes that meant only one thing was on his mind.

He'd ridden into town looking for vengeance.

Sure enough, his steady gaze fell on a man sitting alone in a corner. That man stood and came out from behind his table while the newcomer stomped his feet to the floor. Slowly his hand moved towards his holster then veered upwards until his hand was thrust outwards.

This last action bemused Harlan but when the other man walked across the saloon towards the newcomer with steady clumping footsteps, he leaned forward ready to watch his first saloon confrontation.

The two men stopped and looked each other up and down.

Harlan widened his eyes, ensuring he didn't miss a single detail while he grabbed his pen, but then wished he hadn't bothered when one man lunged in and clapped the other man on the back. Then, with their arms draped over each other's shoulders, they headed to the bar, grinning and chortling to each other as they renewed their acquaintance.

Harlan winced and lowered his head until his forehead was resting on the table, again disappointed in the outcome.

But the irrepressible spirit that had encouraged him to go west in search of authentic adventure to write about won through as he told himself he shouldn't be too eager to see a poker game showdown or a saloon punchup immediately.

So while he waited for the inevitable action to break out, he picked up his book. Marshal Blood was currently dangling over a pit filled with burning coals, a bandit gang was looking on awaiting his demise, and his only available weapon was a toothpick. Blood was surely doomed and even Harlan couldn't see how he'd escape from this predicament.

But as it turned out, Blood did survive, and reading how he did it cheered him into putting his initial disappointment behind him. It was only a matter of time, he told himself confidently, before some real adventure rode into town.

Randolph McDougal shook the reins hurrying the wagon on into Fort Arlen.

An hour ago, he and Fergal O'Brien had shaken off the pig stampede and were free to complete their original intention of heading into town, with Christopher

Tate's information giving them a specific destination of the fort. The anticipation of finally solving the mystery of what was inside their show's main exhibit was making Fergal even more animated than usual.

"Today," he said, punching the air, "we'll actually get to learn the truth about Saint Woody."

"It takes some believing, doesn't it?" Randolph said, enjoying seeing Fergal so happy. "But he can't be a real saint. That must be his name or—"

Fergal slapped a hand over his mouth, silencing him. His stern gaze conveyed that they no longer needed to speculate about the possible answers to the conundrum of who Saint Woody was and what was in the sealed casket he'd made.

Six months ago they'd acquired the casket from another showman, after that showman's unfortunate demise and before they'd learned how to use it. So for the last six months they'd searched for the original creator of the attraction, aiming to solve its mystery.

"Patience, Randolph," Fergal urged.

"I am patient," Randolph said, shaking off Fergal's hand. "You're the one who's so excited."

"Of course I am," Fergal said, grinning wildly. "It'll be a relief to finally find Woody and have ourselves a real attraction. We have a tonic to cure all ills, but frankly our authentic historical exhibits are all trash."

Randolph bit his lip to avoid mentioning his view on Fergal's tonic.

"We did our best."

"Our best isn't good enough, Randolph. Showmen are the future of our great land. Times have been hard, but as life gets easier, people will crave entertainment, and they'll pay for it." Fergal sighed contentedly. "We need to be the ones providing that entertainment, and to do that we need an intriguing main exhibit, something nobody else has, something that'll persuade thousands of people to part with their money."

Randolph smiled. It was rare for Fergal to talk so openly about his vision of what he wanted to achieve.

"You're right, but the treasure of Saint Woody will only do that if there is some real treasure in the casket."

"I believe there is something in there. It may not be the keys to heaven itself, but it will be something interesting." Fergal shrugged. "And if not, we'll make something that looks interesting to put in it, but either way no other showman has a box with spinning circles on the lid that eats money. It'll deliver our fortune one day."

"It's a fine vision, Fergal. But first we have to find a way to get into the fort."

Fergal nodded as he peered ahead at the approaching fort.

"True, so here's our plan. The fort is sure to be heavily guarded, so I'll take the reins. You get on top of the wagon and lie flat and hidden. When I pull up at the gates, I'll distract the guards. You jump off the wagon on to the top of the stockade and over the side, then find somewhere to hide for the rest of the afternoon. When it's dark come out of hiding and sneak around, listening in to the troopers until you get a clue as to where Saint Woody is. You'll have about four hours to learn whatever you can, as when the moon rises I'll pull up beside the gates again. I'll give a coyote howl three times and that's your cue to get over the stockade. Then we'll head out of town to consider what you've learnt."

Randolph pointed. "Or we could just go straight in. The gates are open."

"I guess that'll work too."

As the sleeping guard didn't wake up and challenge them, they rode up to the gates then headed inside. Randolph pulled the wagon up a few yards into the square, then joined Fergal in jumping down.

Aside from a few men sitting around a fire in a corner of the square cooking something on a spit, the square was unoccupied.

The enticing smell of roast pork wafted by as one man left the group and made his steady way over to them. With his dusty jacket flapping open to display a grease-stained shirt that barely covered his rounded belly, he introduced himself as Sergeant Emerson Dodge and in return Fergal announced he'd ridden into town with their traveling show.

"What use has Fort Arlen got for a traveling show?" Emerson asked.

"We have plenty to offer everyone," Fergal said.

"For a start we sell a universal remedy to cure all ills. I'm sure you military men get caught up in plenty of scrapes and it's sure to help soothe away any aches and pains you may have."

Emerson yawned. "As a rule we try to avoid getting into scrapes."

"Then I'm sure I'll have an exhibit that'll fascinate you." Fergal pondered then brightened and raised a finger. "And I have something special that'll interest you military-minded men. I have the original report written by Lieutenant Colonel George Custer on the Battle of the Little Big Horn."

Emerson narrowed his eyes. "Everyone died at that battle. How come Custer managed to write a report on it?"

Fergal's fixed stare didn't waver. "He was a quick writer and he was penning his thoughts right up until the moment of his untimely demise. In fact his last words are most illuminating—"

"Save your breath. Most of the men here aren't regulars. Military reports won't interest them none."

While Fergal frowned, Randolph sighed with relief. He'd never been able to convince Fergal that Custer wouldn't have taken the trouble to pen some profound last words in the midst of a raging lost battle.

"Then perhaps I should move on to my main business in coming here," Fergal said, gesturing towards the wagon. "We have the treasure of Saint Woody."

"There's a saint called Woody?"

"There sure is. And I've heard he's to be found in this very fort."

"Saint Woody?" Emerson furrowed his brow. Then a slow smile spread. "You mean Sergeant Woody?"

Randolph and Fergal both winced.

"Saint . . . Sergeant . . ." Fergal said. "That might explain our confusion."

"Perhaps, but I know one thing for sure: Woody is good with his hands. He could have built yonder box."

"And where might we find Saint . . . Sergeant Woody?"

"He's not here." Emerson scratched his belly. "And I'm kind of too busy right now to go and find him."

Fergal glanced around, taking in the sleeping guard, the men sitting by the fire, then the rest of the square, all of which displayed a general lack of activity.

"Doing what?"

"Our new major is arriving soon to do something or other. Inspect us, I suppose." Emerson stretched. "Got to be ready for that. I've heard that Major Rory Shoot-em-up Mulhoon is a bit keen on military matters."

"I hate to think how he got that name."

Emerson gave a hollow laugh. "You know how some men have the reputation of shooting first and asking questions later? Well, his reputation is worse. He asks the questions first."

"How is that worse?"

"Because he only asks those questions to distract you while he shoots you up."

"And when might—?" Fergal didn't get to finish his question when Emerson's gaze darted up to look over his shoulder.

Randolph turned to see a trooper had drawn his horse to a halt in the open gateway. The newcomer was straight-backed, his buttons shone, and his bushy white mustache bristled as he stared down at the snoring guard.

"What do you think you're doing, man?" he declared at a volume that echoed across the square. But his strident demand didn't wake the guard.

"I reckon that could be Shoot-em-up," Emerson said. "I'll speak to you later when I've seen what he wants."

"Be careful if he asks you a question," Fergal called after him.

Emerson glanced back to offer a smile then sauntered over to the newcomer, who roved his steely gaze away from the sleeping guard to transfix him.

"Major Rory Mulhoon reporting to take command," he declared with a stiff salute. "Who are you?"

Despite knowing Mulhoon's reputation had to be overstated, Emerson still gulped.

"Emerson."

"Emerson . . . ?"

"Emerson Dodge."

Mulhoon swung down from his horse to stand before Emerson. Standing tall he was six inches shorter than the slouching sergeant but he still glared up at

him as if he was looking down on an ant he was
about to crush beneath a well-polished boot.

"Emerson Dodge . . . ?"

Emerson stepped back a pace and raised his hat to
scratch his head.

"Yeah, just Emerson Dod . . . ah, I see what you
mean. I'm Sergeant Emerson Dodge."

"Sergeant Emerson Dodge . . . ?"

"Sorry, you've got me there," Emerson said, with a
slight tremor in his voice. "I ain't got a clue as to what
else you want me to say. That's all the name I've got."

"Then I'll give you a clue. What does a sergeant
say when a major rides into the fort?"

"Howdy?"

"He does not! He gives his superior officer due respect with a crisp military salute, an appropriate military term of respect, and a brief military summation
of the situation."

"Sounds like a good idea." Emerson raised his head
a few inches and waved his hand vaguely beside his
cheek. "Howdy, Shoot-em . . . Rory . . . Major, welcome to this here fort. If you're minded to lose some
money, we've got a game of chuck-a-luck starting up
in an hour, and if you're hungry, we've got a mess of
bacon crisping up a treat."

Mulhoon snorted his breath through his nostrils.

"And what about the gun-runners?"

"We try to avoid those as a rule. They sound like
trouble to me."

"The job of the Plains Cavalry is to seek out trouble and then to deal with it." Mulhoon slapped the revolver at his hip, confirming how he planned to deal with that trouble. "Haven't you read the reports?"

"On what?"

"On the gun-runners! I rooted out a whole nest of those vile spawn at my last fort and I intend to do the same here." Mulhoon fixed Emerson with his stern gaze making his shoulders slump some more. "You are now on report, Sergeant Dodge. You do know what that means, don't you?"

"Not too sure." Emerson pointed at Fergal. "But that man offered to show me one of Lieutenant Colonel George Custer's reports so maybe I could read that and . . ."

Mulhoon's flared nostrils, glaring eyes, and steady tapping of the toe of his boot on the ground persuaded Emerson to stop talking. Then Mulhoon moved his irritated gaze on to Fergal and Randolph.

"And what are—?"

Neither Fergal nor Randolph waited to hear the remainder of the demand. Years of experience of running from trouble told them that nothing good would come from drawing this man's attention to them.

In short order they climbed up on the wagon and trundled it out through the gates.

Randolph didn't waver from his studious consideration of the road beyond the gates, but he still felt Mulhoon's firm gaze boring into him and warming his neck. When they'd passed through the gates and were heading into town he heard further orders ripping out as Mulhoon turned his attention on to the sleeping guard.

"I reckon that new major is about to liven up that sleepy fort," Randolph said as he pulled up the wagon outside the Lazy Sow Saloon.

"He sure will," Fergal said, sighing. "I knew it wouldn't be that easy to meet this Saint . . . Sergeant Woody. From the sounds of it, Emerson could be on report for the rest of his life."

Randolph laughed. "Perhaps we ought to settle down for a long stay, then."

"Agreed, and that means we've got a show to put on." Fergal rubbed his hands while looking around. Several people were roaming down the main road but they all had their heads down or otherwise looked as if they were taken up with their own business. He pointed to the back of the wagon. "Get down quick and be ill before anyone sees you."

Randolph sighed. "What's wrong with me this time?"

"Whatever you want."

Randolph nodded then slipped down off the wagon and around the side to get out of the sight of anyone who happened to look their way. Leaning against the back of the wagon, he listened to Fergal start his sales spiel.

"Roll up, roll up, and be astounded," Fergal cried out, throwing his thin arms wide to display his green waistcoat. Shuffling footfalls sounded as several people gravitated towards the wagon. "And howdy to you, my good man. I reckon you've been waiting for me to ride into town."

"I reckon so too," the potential customer said.

"Excellent." Fergal jumped down from the wagon. "I have many intriguing exhibits of authentic historical memorabilia in my show, but first may I interest you in a tonic? It cures all ills. No injury is so bad, no ailment is so painful, no condition is so—"

"I ain't got nothing wrong with me."

"I'm sure you must have some ills, and just a dollar will make them all disappear."

"Well . . ."

Randolph knew that when a potential customer wavered, it was his cue to appear, so he wandered round to the front of the wagon and milled in with the watching half-dozen people. He saw that the potential buyer of the tonic wore a star and that he wasn't smiling, but that didn't daunt Fergal as he waved towards the group of spectators.

"Perhaps a demonstration might help you to make up your mind. Does anyone here have anything wrong with them?"

Unfortunately two people stepped up but Randolph nudged them aside to reach the front.

"I sure have," he said, casting a fierce glare at the other two that made them back away.

"And what is your affliction?"

Randolph winced. While he'd been waiting to step in he'd been pondering about what they'd have to do to get to see Woody and hadn't put any thought into the illness he could have for Fergal to cure.

"I . . . I can't remember," he murmured, shrugging.

Fergal stared at him, waiting for Randolph to state his ailment, but when Randolph didn't say anything else he brightened.

"Perhaps that's your problem, my good man. Perhaps you've lost your memory and you can't remember nothing."

Randolph nodded, seeing where Fergal was leading him.

"That's it. I can't remember nothing, not my name, not nothing. I don't even know how I got to be in this here town, which I can't remember the name of, seeing as how I can't remember nothing at all."

As his plight made the watching spectators utter a sympathetic murmur, Fergal waggled a bottle of his tonic, making the amber liquid inside sparkle.

"Then maybe if you were to drink a bottle of my tonic to cure all ills you might start remembering again."

"I sure would like to do that, but seeing as I can't remember nothing, I can't remember whether I have any money."

"Then take this tonic for free and see if it works." Fergal held out the bottle.

"That's mighty generous of you."

He uncorked it and steeled himself to take a sip. Many years of being cured by Fergal's tonic meant the rotting polecat taste no longer revolted him, and the churning stomach that used to result rarely plagued him these days, but he still took only a cautious sip.

"And?" Fergal urged.

Randolph rubbed his jaw, looked around at the watching people, then tipped back his hat, letting the moment drag on to increase the tension before the tonic worked its miraculous cure.

"I'm . . . I'm . . . I'm Randolph?" This revelation gathered a smattering of applause. "Yes. I'm Randolph. I remember that."

"That's a good start. Anything more from this most miraculous cure?"

"Yes. I'm remembering more and more." Randolph took another sip. "I'm Randolph McDougal, and this is Fort Arlen, isn't it?" He looked at the lawman, who provided a quick nod.

"Anything else coming back to you?" Fergal asked.

Randolph upended the bottle and downed half the contents.

"Yes. I remember it all now. I'm Randolph McDougal. This is Fort Arlen. You're Fergal . . ." Randolph frowned. "Although why I should remember that I don't know, but I remember everything, and it's all down to your wondrous tonic."

Fergal turned to the watching people with a triumphant smile.

"See? It works. Now would anyone like to test this man's restored memory before my tonic cures their own particular ill, for the perfectly reasonable price of one dollar?"

"I would," the lawman said, stepping up. "Answer me one thing, Randolph McDougal."

"Which is?" Randolph said cautiously, as people were usually too gullible to request further proof.

The lawman leaned forward and lowered his voice.

"What were you doing this morning?"

Randolph gulped when he noticed the lawman's hand stray towards his holster.

"I can't remember that far back yet."

"Then I'll make a few suggestions that might help that returning memory." He turned to Fergal. "You see, I'm investigating a spree of pig rustling. I reckon a seller of a universal remedy that cures people who've lost their memory might remember feeding another tonic with an equally unlikely claim to a hog a few hours ago and making that hog go wild."

Fergal glanced at the wagon, clearly weighing up

how long it'd take them to get on board and hurry out of town before the situation worsened.

"I'm sure we don't know nothing about that."

The lawman slapped a firm hand on both their shoulders and gripped tight.

"Then I suggest you bring a few bottles of your tonic to the law office and we'll see if it helps you remember exactly what it was you were doing this morning."

Chapter Four

*T*he explosion tore the cell door off, sending it hurtling across the law office.

Garth waved away the dust and smoke as he walked to freedom.

"Where did you hide that dynamite, Rick?" he asked.

Rick just winked as he reclaimed his gun from the armory then tossed Garth his weapon.

"And now," he said, "we just have to find a way to make Blood rue the day he ever took on the Hunter brothers."

Garth grunted that he agreed. They headed to the door, but when Rick threw it open he saw that a man was sitting on the boardwalk. He was rubbing his head, the explosion clearly having

39

caught him unawares as he was about to enter the law office.

He was thin and wore a green waistcoat. He looked up at them and offered them a smile.

"I'm Fergal O'Brien," he said. "I was looking for Marshal Blood."

Rick sneered then dragged Fergal to his feet.

"Any friend of Marshal Blood's is an enemy of mine," he said, smirking as an idea took hold, "and you have just volunteered to be a hostage."

Marshal Ed Buckley settled back in his chair.

Now that he'd locked his prisoners in a cell to stew awhile before he questioned them, and enjoyed his dinner of a thick slice of well-cooked ham, he was free to resume reading his Marshal Blood tale.

He was more contented than he had been when he'd put down the book. A good meal caught by his own hand and his first arrests of the year might not have been achievements that would have satisfied Marshal Blood, but it was enough to please Buckley.

But he'd read only another page when he noticed a shadow on the window. He raised himself to see a man was reading the wanted poster by the door.

"It's all go today," he said to himself as he headed to the door to investigate.

He opened the door to find a morose-looking young man glaring at the poster with ill-concealed disgust.

He introduced himself and learned that the man was Harlan Finchley then asked him what he wanted.

"I was looking at your wanted *poster*," Harlan said, pointing and putting enough aggrieved emphasis into his tone to let Buckley know something about that poster annoyed him. "Is this all you've got?"

"I run a quiet town."

"Yeah, but I was hoping for something more exciting than this . . . this . . ." Harlan waved his arms vaguely as he searched for the right words. "Nothing happens in Fort Arlen. There just aren't no outlaws here."

"We've got enough of those." Buckley stabbed a finger on the wanted poster.

"Well, I've got to say that man is the ugliest looking critter I've ever seen with those small eyes, flat nose and wide nostrils." Harlan narrowed his eyes and cocked his head to one side. "He looks like a pig."

"He is a pig," Buckley said, tearing down the poster. "He's the only witness I have to our terrible spree of pig rustling, and one that I might just have solved."

Harlan stared at Buckley, his eyes wide with incredulity.

"Is there another Fort Arlen," he murmured, "where there's real trouble and the law office doesn't display wanted posters of pigs?"

Although Buckley was usually quick to complain that nothing exciting ever happened in Fort Arlen, hearing this sentiment from a newcomer brought out a swelling of pride in his town he never knew he had.

"This town is mighty fine just the way it is."

"No offense meant. I just didn't think the town where Marshal Blood is supposed to be a lawman would be this . . . this sleepy."

"So," Buckley said, folding his arms to avoid feeling guilty at the irony of his statement, "you're someone who wastes away his life reading Marshal Blood dime novels, are you?"

"Sure am, and I know one thing for sure. Blood's the kind of lawman who wouldn't waste his time on no pig rustling."

"Are you sure?" Buckley snorted, irritated by the implied insult. He drew himself up to his full height. "Who do you think they base Marshal Blood on?"

Harlan looked Buckley's short and rounded form up and down, shock making him stumble back a pace.

"You?" he murmured aghast.

"In the flesh. The real life, inspiration and embodiment of the fictional lawman Marshal Colt T Blood."

"But . . ." Harlan shook himself, put a hand to his heart, took deep breaths, then got himself under control and reached out to shake Buckley's hand.

Buckley had only meant his comment as a joke to get some fun out of Harlan's arrogant attitude, but seeing the unquestioning adoration in his eyes, something he'd never seen before in anyone's eyes, gave him an unexpected comforting feeling.

Swaggering slightly, he headed back into his office, beckoning Harlan to follow him in.

"I sure am the real Marshal Blood," he said as he sat at his desk. "Ask me anything you like about my life and I'll prove it."

Harlan stood before his desk, waving his hands as he pondered on his first question.

"I've got thousands, but first . . . I enjoyed the way you wiped out that bandit gang when you were searching for the lost city of gold. But how did you work out the missing part of the map was hidden in a locket in the bandit leader's saddlebag? The story never explained that."

"I haven't finished read—" Buckley winced when from the corner of his eye he noticed the orange cover of the unfinished book on his desk. Before Harlan could see it he nudged the book into the open top drawer with his elbow then closed the drawer. "Which story is that?"

"You mean you don't know?"

"Well, I don't know for sure what they put in the books. I'm too busy catching the real outlaws to waste my time reading stories about myself. But I do know that what I do in the real situations is usually different to the way they write it up."

"That's what I thought and that's why I've come

here to find out the full truth." Harlan gestured at the screwed-up wanted poster. "So answer me this—how can the real Marshal Blood cope with mundane matters like pig rustlers?"

"Most of what happens in a lawman's life *is* mundane, but there's one thing I can always rely on. When you've got a reputation like mine, Marshal Colt T Blood just has to bide his time, and before long trouble is sure to ride into town." Buckley raised his eyebrows. "What do you think the T stands for?"

"I've never found that out. I've read all the books and it's never been . . ."—Harlan laughed when he saw Buckley smile—"and there's that trademark humor I came to see firsthand, and to write about."

"Write?"

"Yeah. Maybe one day I'll have the courage to create my own characters but right now I want to write a Marshal Blood adventure. Beadle's dime novel series is written by many different writers so I reckon they'll publish my story, provided it's authentic enough, and the only place I can get that authentic flavor is where the action is, Fort Arlen."

Buckley blew out his cheeks. "Then I wish you luck."

"I don't need no luck. I've found the real Marshal Blood. I just have to follow you for a few days and I'll get to see gunfights and saloon brawls and bank raids and—"

"Now just hold on a minute there," Buckley said, raising a hand. "That's not the way it happens in real life. Those there dime novels you've been reading cover just a small part of being a lawman. Most of what goes on is careful investigating here in the office."

"I know, and that's what I want to see—the things nobody else writes about. I can't be the only one who wants to know what life for a real lawman in the real West is like. Please, let me follow you. Let me see everything. Let me write about the truth."

Buckley gulped. He'd enjoyed the adoration Harlan had given him after he'd accepted his harmless piece of subterfuge as the truth, but now the conversation had strayed into uncomfortable territory.

Although Harlan claimed he wanted to see the truth, Buckley reckoned in reality he wanted to see a version of the action-packed adventures he'd read about in the dime novels. So he was sure to be disappointed if he spent time with a lawman whose most exciting incident this year had been filling a runaway hog full of lead—tasty as it had been—and catching two suspected pig rustlers.

Buckley shook his head. "Sorry, Harlan. Bearing in mind the kind of danger I face every day, I couldn't risk an innocent citizen's life by letting him trail me. I wouldn't be a good lawman if I did that, would I?"

"I guess not." Harlan frowned then offered a tentative smile. "So let me follow one of your investigations from a safe distance. I'll be writing a lot of the time so I won't be in your way. Please."

Buckley considered the pleading young man and as he couldn't think of any more excuses right now to dissuade him from his plan, he shooed him away to the door.

"I'll think about it," he said, nodding towards the small jailhouse at the back the law office. "Now, you've got to go. I've got some suspects to question."

"Then I'll leave you to your questioning, Marshal Blood . . . Marshal Buckley. I'll see you again tomorrow and I do so hope you'll let me accompany you."

Harlan stared at him with his mouth partly open and his eyes burning with admiration then scurried outside.

Buckley looked through the window to confirm that Harlan was heading across the road towards the hotel then opened the top drawer of his desk and withdrew his book.

"Now," he said to himself, "let me see how *I* wiped out those bandits."

"What you listening to?" Randolph asked, stretching himself on his cot.

By the cell door, Fergal gestured for Randolph to be quiet. He listened at the door for a few moments longer then sighed and headed over to sit on his cot.

"A mighty interesting conversation was going on in the law office."

"About Saint Woody?"

"Nothing about him, but I reckon we've already solved that problem. We just have to wait for Sergeant Emerson Dodge to tell us where he is and then we'll get all the answers we've been searching for."

Randolph gestured around at the cell. "You're forgetting something, Fergal. We won't get to see that sergeant. We're stuck in a cell, under arrest for pig rustling, and I reckon that's a pretty serious crime around these parts."

"Don't worry about that. I'm getting an idea as to how we get out of here."

"How?"

Fergal provided a devious smile that Randolph had seen many times before and which told him that whatever thoughts were going on in Fergal's mind they were sure to test his principles, and probably the speed of his gun-hand too.

But with Fergal offering no further explanation and with nothing else to occupy their minds, they lay back on their cots and idled away the afternoon.

Sundown was reddening the cell when the marshal finally opened the door of the small jailhouse and came in.

"All right," he said, looking at them through the cell bars. "Have you two drank enough of your tonic to remember everything you've done today?"

"If you're going to be sarcastic," Randolph said, sitting up, "we won't answer none of your questions."

"You have the right to ignore me, but that won't stop me asking questions, and I reckon I'll start at the beginning." Buckley looked at each man in turn. "So, how long have you been pig rustling?"

"We aren't pig rustlers," Fergal said. "We run a traveling show, displaying exhibits of authentic historical memorabilia and selling a universal remedy to cure all ills."

Buckley snorted. "A universal remedy that works so well it cured your partner of his amnesia several seconds after he—"

"Randolph is right. Sarcasm won't help none here."

"Then what will get answers from you two?"

Fergal rolled his feet down to the floor and lowered his voice to provide an honest tone.

"We have nothing to answer to. The truth is we were on our way into town when this poor farmer begged us to help him. I fed my tonic to his sick pigs, but unfortunately some of those hogs took exception to the medicine and broke loose."

Buckley nodded, walking back and forth before the cell door.

"Obliged you've decided to talk, but that story doesn't explain the coincidence of how you then just happened to visit the very fort where one of those poor animals ran to."

Fergal sniffed, although the pleasant aroma of sizzling ham had long since drifted away.

"How will you prove we had a sinister intent after you've eaten the evidence?"

Buckley winced. "I have a strong enough case already. I have a witness who saw you enrage his hogs with a tonic then run away, witnesses who saw a hog rampaging round the fort, the remains of a tasty stew, and witnesses who saw you head into the fort."

Fergal stretched back on his cot. He glanced at Randolph and winked then considered his fingernails before buffing them on his jacket.

"And this lawman reckons that's enough evidence to convict us of attempted pig rustling, does he?"

"He sure does."

"And how might a lawman other than yourself conduct himself in this situation . . . a lawman like Marshal Colt T Blood, for instance?"

Buckley narrowed his eyes. "What do you mean?"

"I mean I heard what that young man Harlan said out there in the law office. He's somehow got it into his head that you are the inspiration behind Marshal Blood, the famous fictional lawman."

"But I am."

Fergal looked Buckley up and down, then chuckled.

"Of course you're not. Somehow I don't think *Marshal Blood and the Pig Rustlers* would make a good title for a dime novel."

"I don't care what you think."

"You should." Fergal smiled. "I saw the book on your desk. I know you told Harlan you were Marshal Blood because you secretly wish you were him, instead of being a bored lawman in a sleepy town where the most excitement you get is shooting up runaway hogs."

Buckley snorted, his firm jaw and slowness in responding confirming Fergal had correctly divined his attitude.

"All right. I accept that. I'm not happy my life isn't as exciting as it is for the lawmen in the dime novels, but that doesn't change my duty as the legally sworn-in marshal of Fort Arlen."

"You can accept that real life isn't like it is in the stories, but what about Harlan? He idolizes you, but if he stays and writes his Marshal Blood adventure based on your sleepy life in this sleepy town, you'll destroy his dreams, won't you?"

"I'll find an excuse that'll persuade him to move on with those dreams intact."

"But can you do that? He might still find out the truth . . . somehow."

Buckley narrowed his eyes. "I understand where you're going with this threat. You want a deal. I let you out of this cell or you'll tell Harlan the truth and destroy his dreams."

"I want a deal but not that one." Fergal spread his hands and treated Buckley to his most devious smile.

"I'm a showman, and I plan to make all of Harlan's dreams come true."

Harlan Finchley looked out of his hotel room window and onto the road below, hoping to see the trouble that Buckley had promised arrived every day, but this morning the town was as quiet as it had been yesterday.

From his elevated position he could see into the fort at the end of the road. Inside, the troopers were more animated than they had been yesterday. Many had lined up in the center of the square to be inspected. Others were dashing around cleaning.

Windows were being wiped, horses were being washed down, and some men were even scrubbing the wooden stockade. But all the effort looked organized and trouble-free.

Movement nearer by caught Harlan's attention and he looked to the road to see the wagon that had been sitting outside the Lazy Sow Saloon all night was heading down the road away from him. He watched the wagon until it had left town then roved his gaze down to the road to see Marshal Ed Buckley had emerged from the law office and was embarking on a leisurely patrol.

Harlan decided this was as good a time as any to find out if he would let him stay, or if he would crush his hopes.

Although he was prepared for the worst, when he

hurried down to the road and caught up with Buckley, he found the lawman in good cheer.

"Howdy there, young Harlan," Buckley declared, gesturing for him to walk along the boardwalk with him.

Harlan matched Buckley's slow pace and adopted his posture of holding his hands behind his back. Despite Buckley's cheerful demeanor he forced himself to remain calm in case of bad news.

"Have you thought any more about my request?" he asked, his voice cracking with a tremor.

"I sure have." Buckley rubbed his chin, looking aloft as if he was thinking through a great problem. "And I've decided . . . you can follow me, but—"

"Yeehaw!" Harlan shouted, punching the air. Then he reached over and shook Buckley's hand. "You won't regret this. I'll write the greatest ever Marshal Blood adventure and make you a living legend—not that you're not one already—but after I've written about the way your life really is, people will think you even more legendary, if that's possible. My tale will be—"

"Harlan, stop babbling and calm down."

Harlan took a deep breath. "Sorry, Marshal. I'm just so excited."

"I can see that. Now listen to me carefully. You can follow me for one adventure . . . investigation. But you will stay back and out of danger when I tell you to. After I've concluded that investigation, you will write your Marshal Blood adventure then leave town."

Harlan lowered his head. Elation at having his request accepted and disappointment at being told to leave town afterwards vied to control his emotions. Elation won.

"I agree to your terms, Marshal. I did only request that I could follow you for one investigation and I'm grateful you've accepted." He rubbed his hands and glanced along the deserted road. "So how long do you reckon it'll be before trouble rides into town?"

Buckley paced to a halt then joined Harlan in looking along the road. He turned, taking in the closed fort, the closed saloon, the closed mercantile until he'd turned completely around, by which time a man hurrying down the boardwalk towards them drew his attention. The man was tall and solidly built, and intriguingly his expression was grim.

"Like I told you," Buckley said, "Marshal Blood never has to wait long for trouble to present itself . . . and it could well be arriving now."

To Harlan the approaching man didn't look like trouble. On the contrary, when he reached them he removed his hat, ran it nervously through his hands then pointed out of town with a shaking hand.

"I need help, Marshal," he said.

"What's the problem?"

"My name's Randolph McDougal. I run this here

traveling show with my partner Fergal O'Brien, but yesterday we had a heap of trouble from these two varmints Rick and Garth Hunter."

The mention of these names made Buckley's eyes widen before he got himself under control with a firm nod.

"Notorious outlaws indeed," he murmured.

"I'd heard you'd had plenty of run-ins with the errant Hunter brothers, but this time they've kidnapped Fergal and stolen our wagon from outside the Lazy Sow Saloon."

"I saw that wagon head out of town," Harlan said.

"Did you see Rick and Garth driving it?" Randolph asked.

"No."

Randolph sighed, his low utterance sounding almost relieved, but Harlan put that down to his nervousness. Randolph rummaged in his pocket and produced a note, which he handed to Buckley.

"Rick left this message."

Buckley took the note and read it, nodding with his face set in a grave expression.

"This is terrible news."

"Can I read it?" Harlan asked.

"No," Buckley said, tucking the note in his pocket. "This is now evidence, but it appears the Hunter brothers are holding Randolph's partner hostage. Either I agree to meet them, or they'll kill him."

"That's terrible. What're you going to do, Marshal? Raise a posse? Go to the—"

Buckley raised a hand, silencing him. "I told you, Harlan. You have to keep that enthusiasm of yours under control and you must keep out of my way. This is a serious matter and a man's life is at stake."

Harlan accepted this rebuke with a quick nod then stood back to see how Buckley conducted the investigation, already memorizing every detail so he could write them up later. But it was Randolph who offered the first suggestion.

"I'm an experienced tracker, Marshal," he said. "I should be able to follow our wagon and find out where the Hunter brothers have taken Fergal."

"That's a mighty fine starting point," Buckley said. "So don't worry, Randolph. From what I've heard so far I reckon I will be able to rescue Fergal or my name isn't Marshal Blood . . . Marshal Buckley."

Chapter Five

"*C*an you see anything?" Marshal Blood asked.

"Not yet, but trust me," Randolph McDougal said, his lively but concerned eyes betraying his burning desire to save his partner's life.

He dropped to his knees to consider the rutted road then ran his fingers over the dirt until his fingertips settled inside one particular set of wheel tracks. Then he stood and set off for his horse.

To Blood's unskilled eyes the tracks had looked no different to any other wheel tracks. But he was mindful of Randolph's last words to him and so, without comment, he followed Randolph to his horse and out of town.

Without detours or unnecessary delays, Randolph kept track of the trail he'd picked up, a trail that ultimately led to an abandoned shack five miles out of town.

The stolen wagon stood outside, the sight making Randolph firm his jaw with pride and making Blood draw his gun.

"Stay back, Randolph," he said, stepping forward. "Marshal Blood works alone."

"Not this time," Randolph said, drawing his gun as he joined him.

Blood was minded to argue, but Randolph had a determined gleam in his eye that said this was one argument he would never win.

"All right," he said using his usual quiet and authoritative voice, "here's my plan to free Fergal, your stalwart . . ."

"What's stalwart mean?" Randolph asked, peering over Harlan's shoulder at his writing.

"It means Fergal is trustworthy and dependable."

"Wait until you meet him," Randolph murmured to himself then raised his voice. "You been doing this writing for long?"

"I've been thinking about it for years, but only started seriously about an hour ago." Harlan waved the paper. "I'm writing up everything the marshal does for a Marshal Blood dime novel."

Randolph looked over their covering boulder at the

shack, which was one hundred yards away and was roofless with collapsed walls.

"It sure will be interesting to find myself being written about in a real dime novel." Randolph smiled then hardened his expression to a frown and placed a hand on Harlan's arm to ensure he didn't write any more. "But I'll only find it interesting if we get Fergal out of there alive."

"That's right," Marshal Buckley said turning away from his consideration of the shack, "so don't you go forgetting that this isn't a story, Harlan. We're about to take on two vicious outlaws to try to save a man's life. If things go wrong, innocent men could die here."

Harlan nodded and put on a suitably somber expression.

"I know. I won't do any more writing until I know Fergal is safe."

Buckley accepted this promise with a curt nod then ordered Harlan to stay behind cover while he and Randolph made their way over to the shack.

On the count of three they emerged from behind the covering boulder and hurried with their heads down to the next nearest cover of an oak. Then they snaked from a mound of earth to another boulder, to another tree before pausing for breath twenty yards from the shack.

Randolph glanced back to confirm Harlan hadn't followed them and was keeping his head down.

"What's the plan now?" he asked, drawing his gun and punching in a final bullet.

Buckley looked at the gun, shaking his head.

"Remember this rescue's not for real. You can't go in there a-shooting in all directions. Someone might get hurt."

"I know, but we have to make this look realistic."

Buckley pointed towards Harlan's position.

"He's too far away to see what happens next, and besides, he doesn't want realistic. He wants to write a dime novel. So just follow my lead."

Randolph chuckled. "Obliged to you for your noble aid in freeing Fergal from the clutches of those terrible brothers, Rick and Garth Hunter."

Buckley gave Randolph a long glare that told him he found nothing amusing about this situation, then stood.

"Rick and Garth Hunter," he shouted, "this is Marshal Bloo . . . Marshal Ed Buckley. You have five seconds to come out reaching for the sky, or I'll be a-coming in to get you."

Randolph stood, sighing. "Do lawmen in dime novels really say things like that?"

"Marshal Blood does."

"Then how does he ever survive to appear in another book if he gives the outlaws a five-second warning that he's coming in?"

"He survives because he's the lawman." Buckley began pacing towards the house, heading towards the lowest length of wall. "One . . ."

Randolph followed him. By the count of three he saw Fergal over the four-foot-high wall, sitting against the wall at the far end of the shack.

Fergal waved and then, while smiling, put a hand to his throat and a pointed finger to his head in a mime of being held at gunpoint.

Buckley reached five then hurried to the house. He vaulted over the wall then drew his gun. When he'd taken three more paces to take himself out of Harlan's view, he shot over the side of the wall away from Fergal.

Randolph joined him and loosed off a couple of shots beyond the wall before Buckley swung round and gestured at him to stop firing.

"Got to make it appear like a pitched battle," Randolph said, "to give Harlan plenty to write about."

"Then stop firing. Harlan knows that Marshal Blood always hits what he aims at and never needs no second shot to dispose of the outlaws."

"And now that you've shot up my kidnappers," Fergal said, standing, "I have to say I'm mighty glad you saved me from a terrible—"

"Quit the joking, you two," Buckley said. "I only agreed to do this to help Harlan, but that doesn't mean I'm proud of myself for play-acting."

"You should be. That was mighty brave of you coming over the wall after telling the Hunter brothers where you were."

Buckley pointed at Fergal with his jaw set firm.

"Any more comments like that and you'll be back in a cell."

Fergal narrowed his eyes. "You can't go back on our deal."

"I'm not. Our deal was I'd let you out of a cell in exchange for you giving Harlan something to write about. I've done that, but that doesn't mean I've proved you aren't pig rustlers. If I ever do prove it, I will arrest you, and don't say you'll tell Harlan because I have my duty to discharge whether it destroys his dreams or not."

Fergal opened his mouth to utter a retort, but then closed it, turned on his heel and ran for the open doorway.

"Is he running away?" Buckley said, turning to Randolph.

"Fergal is *always* running away, but I reckon this time he's just being rescued." Randolph gestured around at the deserted shack. "And I reckon he's got the right idea. We don't want to spend too much time in here, what with these dead bodies littering up the place."

"I guess you're right. Harlan can't get to see in here." Buckley turned to follow Fergal. "And I've had more than enough of this."

Buckley and Randolph followed Fergal outside to see he was cowering beside the wagon while peering at the shack, providing a good impression of how he would react if this situation were real.

While walking over to him, Buckley beckoned to Harlan, confirming with a thumbs-up signal that the situation was under control and that it was safe for him to approach.

While they stood beside the wagon and waited for him, Randolph looked back towards Fort Arlen and noted that a line of riders was approaching, the gunfire perhaps having attracted their attention. As yet they were too far away for him to see who they were.

"Did you kill them both?" Harlan asked when he arrived.

"Sure did," Buckley said. "I shot up Rick and Randolph got Garth."

"I wish I could have seen that." Harlan moved to go towards the house but Buckley grabbed his arm.

"Where do you think you're going?" he asked.

"To see the dead men."

"You don't want to see that, Harlan."

"But how else am I supposed to write about the gunfight and its aftermath if I can't see the bodies?"

"That mean you've never seen a shot-up man before?"

"No."

"Then don't let them be the first. It's not a fit sight for nobody, and besides, no one wants to read about gunshot wounds in a dime novel."

"I guess so."

Harlan's shoulders slumped and when Buckley released his arm he lowered his head and slouched to the wagon against which he leaned.

"You don't seem that happy," Buckley said.

"I'm not, I guess." Harlan raised his head and offered a brief smile. "I mean I'm happy that Randolph got his partner out of there alive, but it was all over too quickly. I've only written eight pages so far and that gunfight will get me only another ten or so. How am I supposed to turn one shootout into a whole Marshal Blood adventure?"

"Not got a clue but then again I'm no writer. I'm just a lawman who people write about, and as I told you, real-life investigations are different and often shorter." Buckley shrugged when Harlan opened his mouth to complain some more. "But I'd suggest you need to take this as a starting point then use your imagination to embellish the events a little."

"I could, but can't I just follow you until I'm sure there are no loose ends? In a Marshal Blood adventure this would just be the start of the story." Harlan spoke faster as his enthusiasm returned. "Blood would think he only has to rescue a kidnapped man, but then he'd find out someone else had been taken, so he didn't wipe out the whole Hunter gang and—"

"Now hold on a minute there, Harlan," Buckley snapped, raising a hand. "We agreed you'd follow me on one investigation. And we've had it. Fergal got kidnapped, I rescued him. That's the end of the investigation and there are no loose ends."

Harlan began to lower his head, but from over by the back of the wagon, Fergal spoke up.

"Wait! Harlan's right. There is a loose end. Perhaps you didn't track down all the Hunter gang, after all."

Harlan looked up with hope lighting his eyes while Buckley swirled round to face Fergal with his eyes flaring.

"What?"

"Our prize exhibit is the treasure of Saint Woody," Fergal said, pointing into the wagon.

"There's a saint called Woody?" Harlan asked.

"There sure is, except while Rick and Garth held me at gunpoint, someone broke into our wagon and stole it."

Randolph temporarily forgot the crisis wasn't for real and moved to the back of the wagon to look inside, but when Fergal winked at him he shook himself then let his mouth open wide to show how shocked he was.

"Fergal's right! Our priceless treasure has been stolen."

"I reckon," Fergal said, "this has to be the work of the third Hunter brother Frank."

"I thought he was dead," Randolph said, getting into the spirit of Fergal's tale.

"Obviously he's not and from what I know of him, Frank Hunter was the worst of a bad bunch."

Harlan rubbed his hands with glee. "I knew it! The adventure is only just beginning."

Buckley didn't join in Harlan's good cheer as he grabbed Fergal's arm and dragged him away from the wagon.

"What are you doing?" he snapped in a low voice when he was out of Harlan's earshot.

"If you're going to manipulate the terms of our agreement," Fergal said, smiling, "so can I."

"Why?"

"To give Harlan what he wants. He wasn't content with the little adventure I staged for him, so he wasn't going to leave you alone until he had something more. I'm giving him something more."

"I am not traipsing around pretending to search for your missing exhibit when it's in the back of your wagon."

"You don't need to traipse around." Fergal pointed back down the trail where the approaching riders were now clearly discernible as being cavalrymen with the new major riding up front. "You just need to talk to Major Mulhoon. We've come to town to see Sergeant Woody and if you could arrange for us to do that, as part of your ongoing investigation, I'm sure it'll help us *find* the exhibit very quickly."

Buckley narrowed his eyes. "That was your plan all along, wasn't it? You weren't content with just getting out of jail. You staged all this just to get my help in speaking to Woody."

Fergal pouted. "You wound me with your lack of trust. But not to worry. We only want to see Woody.

Then I'll relate a story about how we tracked down Frank Hunter and reclaimed our stolen treasure that'll thrill Harlan enough to let him fill a dozen dime novels, and to leave you alone."

Buckley looked at the troopers, confirming they were heading towards them, then kicked at the earth. He sighed, then provided a quick nod.

"All right, I'll do it, but that's all I do. Whether Major Mulhoon helps you or not, I'm finished with this play-acting."

"But of course."

They all turned to watch the riders approach. Riding behind Major Mulhoon was Sergeant Emerson Dodge, now dressed in a crisp shiny-buttoned uniform as were the rest of the troopers.

"What can we do for you?" Buckley asked when the riders had drawn up.

"I heard shooting and came to investigate," Mulhoon said, peering around eagerly. "I only ever go in one direction when there's gunfire."

Randolph noted Emerson looked skyward and winced as if he'd heard this sentiment too many times recently.

"The situation is under control," Buckley reported, receiving an aggrieved grunt from Mulhoon.

"Except for my missing property," Fergal prompted.

Buckley glared at him, suggesting he wouldn't take up the offer to act on Fergal's request, but then his shoulders slumped and he shuffled round to face Mulhoon.

"It'd help to tie up the loose ends here," he said wearily, "if we could speak with one of your men, a Sergeant Woody."

Mulhoon sighed. "It'd help me too if I could speak with that man. It appears he's gone missing. So what has he done now?"

Buckley held a hand out to Fergal, inviting him to talk, then shot him a narrowed-eyed glare that said he'd done everything he would do to help him.

"He built a casket we now own," Fergal said as Buckley headed off to join Harlan. "Nobody knows how to open it, except Woody, but that's the least of our problems now that the soul-surviving member of the notorious Hunter gang has stolen it."

"And how big is this box?" Mulhoon asked, fingering his whiskers.

"Big?" Fergal murmured, taken aback by the odd question. He got himself under control with a shrug then gestured as he spoke, miming a large box. "About six-feet long and—"

"Gun-runners!" Mulhoon said, slapping a fist into his other palm. "I knew it."

"I never said anything about gun-running."

"You didn't need to. All the evidence points to it. A man on the last train to arrive in town was suspected of harboring a consignment of rifles. Then Sergeant

Woody, the man who was in charge of the armory, goes missing. Now a casket he built gets stolen by a notorious outlaw gang, and the casket is big enough to store guns in a place where only one man can reach them." Mulhoon slapped his revolver. "I see a pattern of gun-running, and the only way to stop this getting out of control is with hot lead."

"I am most grateful for any help you may provide in finding Sergeant Woody." Fergal offered his most ingratiating smile while Mulhoon glared around with a hand on his revolver as if he was already on the verge of rooting out those imagined gun-runners.

When Mulhoon had finished his slow consideration of the surroundings, he fixed Emerson with his stern gaze.

"Sergeant Dodge, I task you with noting the details from these men. I'll return to base to put together an armed team of able men—assuming I can find any—ready to capture Woody and his gun-runners."

Emerson shook his head. "Woody ain't no gun-runner."

Mulhoon bristled with indignation. "Woody ain't no gun-runner . . . ?"

"Woody ain't no gun-runner, *sir*," Emerson murmured, while waving a hand vaguely beside his forehead.

With a crisp military salute, Mulhoon swung his horse away. Emerson waited until Mulhoon was riding back to the fort before turning to Fergal.

"I'm sorry your property got stolen by a notorious outlaw," he said, "but Woody is a good man and I'm sure he's not behind anything like gun-running."

"I hope so too," Fergal said, "but all we want is to meet him, and to get our exhibit back."

Emerson nodded, his lively eyes confirming he'd understood Fergal's implication.

"I've heard all about you and your devious ways. I reckon the exhibit is still sitting in the back of your wagon and this tale of a notorious outlaw gang was just a ruse to get me to tell you where Woody is."

Fergal considered Emerson then looked over to check that Buckley and Harlan couldn't hear him before he spoke again.

"Just tell me how I can find him."

"I could, but I'm about to spend so much time chasing after these phantom gun-runners that the major's obsessed with, I haven't got the time to talk to you."

Fergal offered a sympathetic smile. "Has he changed life in the fort, then?"

"You wouldn't believe how much," Emerson said with an exasperated sigh. "He has men polishing buttons, polishing horses, polishing rocks, polishing the wooden stockade. Apparently on his last assignment he tracked down a gang of gun-runners and that went down well with his superiors. He reckons a promotion is in the offing. So he's determined to find more gun-runners and that means the man just can't be reasoned with."

Fergal rubbed his chin while he pondered then lowered his voice to a conspiratorial tone.

"Then maybe you should get rid of him so your life can return to its normal sleepy pattern."

"It's a pleasant thought." Emerson looked at the departing major. "But how could anyone get rid of a man like Major Mulhoon?"

Fergal snorted a low laugh. "The question you should ask doesn't involve how, but the simpler one of, what's it going to cost?"

Chapter Six

"*I*'*ve got me a bullet already loaded,*" *Marshal Blood muttered through gritted teeth,* "*and it's got Frank Hunter's name on it.*"

"*If you want me to carve some names of my own,*" *Fergal said, nodding,* "*you just have to ask.*"

Blood considered Fergal, an honorable man he'd come to trust.

"*I know. I welcome your help, and one thing is already certain to me: The key to finding Frank is to find the treasure of . . .*"

Harlan Finchley settled back in his chair, a thought coming to him. He pondered some more until a small voice in his mind told him that the thought was a good one.

71

So far, as he'd written his burgeoning Marshal Blood tale, he'd felt unfocused. Earlier he'd realized that was because the story lacked a title.

But an intriguing idea had just come to him, so he shuffled through the twenty pages he'd written so far to reach the first page.

He considered his opening lines, pondered some more, and finally decided his thought for a title to his first Marshal Blood adventure was the right one.

So with a flourish he wrote in large capital letters at the top of the page:

THE TREASURE OF SAINT WOODY *by Harlan Finchley.*

* * *

"Are you sure Emerson actually knows where Sergeant Woody is?" Randolph asked after the guard had accepted their explanation that they wanted to see Sergeant Dodge.

"He claims he does," Fergal said as the guard waved them on through the fort gates, "and we have no choice but to trust him."

"And to do his biding."

"Relax. All we have to do for him is this one little thing."

Randolph sighed as he peered around the fort square.

Sun-up was still an hour away and although Major Mulhoon's new regime meant more animated activity was taking place than when they'd visited two days ago, he was pleased to note the armory wasn't guarded, making their next task easier.

"I'm surprised you sound so confident when that one little thing is to get rid of Major Mulhoon."

"I'm sure it can be done. Now quit worrying. We've got some gun-running to do."

They trundled across the square and drew up outside the mess hall, the nearest building to the armory, then alighted.

Fergal drew the attention of the nearest trooper, who then hurried off to fetch Emerson.

By the time Emerson arrived Randolph had wandered casually to the rear of the wagon where he sat on the back and with seemingly idle curiosity watched the troopers mill around.

Fergal struck up a conversation with Emerson. Randolph couldn't hear what they said but he presumed Fergal was employing his usual talent to distract with some outrageous claims about his tonic. Sure enough the troopers guarding the armory murmured to each other then gravitated towards the front of the wagon to see what Fergal was saying and doing.

When everybody was out of Randolph's sight he wasted no time in nonchalantly pacing away from the wagon and into the armory.

Randolph hadn't known what he'd find inside, but the only contents in the rank-smelling room were five piled-up crates. He hurried over to them to see that each crate had been labeled as containing one hundred rifles.

"I guess five crates will do for a spot of gun-running," he said to himself, experimentally hefting one side of the first crate. It was lighter than he'd expected it would be, but then again he'd never wondered how heavy one hundred rifles would be.

He dragged the box to the door and looked out at the square, confirmed that nobody was looking his way, then maneuvered it to the wagon.

Another ten minutes of teeth-gritting effort later, all five crates were safely stowed inside the back of the wagon beside the treasure of Saint Woody. Then, while whistling to himself, he sauntered around to the front of the wagon and milled in with the troopers.

He caught Fergal's eye and so Fergal stopped extolling the virtues of his tonic and drew Emerson aside. With nothing interesting to listen to any more, the rest of the troopers disbanded.

"So what exactly is your plan?" Emerson asked as Randolph joined them.

"It might be better if you didn't ask," Fergal said.

"But it won't be anything that'll cause more trouble than having Major Mulhoon in charge, will it?"

"Of course not," Fergal said with an aggrieved tone Randolph had heard many times before and which he always reserved for his most outrageous lies. "You want me to remove Major Mulhoon before you'll tell me how I can find Sergeant Woody, so I will."

"But how? I can't see how a mere tonic seller who runs a traveling show can get rid of a trigger-happy military man like Major Mulhoon."

Fergal winked. "As I said to someone else recently, by making all of Major Mulhoon's dreams come true."

"This is utter trash," Marshal Ed Buckley said, throwing Harlan's story on to his desk.

"Why?" Harlan murmured, aghast. He had been nervous about letting Buckley see what he'd written, but had thought he would still approve of the unfinished tale.

"This bit about me trusting the honorable Fergal O'Brien." Buckley stabbed a finger against the page, then turned it round for Harlan to see. "Where did you get that idea?"

Harlan read the offending passage, then shrugged.

"But you do trust him, don't you?"

"I trust him about as far as I . . ." Buckley took several deep breaths. "Let's just say I'm keeping an open mind and making my own decisions."

Harlan smiled. "You really are a man alone. I'll change that section. What about the rest?"

Buckley sighed. "I suppose it's readable. You're just explaining everything that happened yesterday from your viewpoint, so I guess that raging gun battle you described is fairly well done. Although I do think it was unlikely Rick Hunter would have suspended Fergal over a pit of rattlesnakes, then taken the trouble to have Garth use a candle to burn through the rope that was holding him up."

"You didn't let me go inside the shack to see what state Fergal was in when you rescued him, so like you suggested, I used my imagination to embellish the events."

"Which was a good idea, except I'd have liked an explanation of how Rick and Garth collected the rattlesnakes and how they managed to dig out a ten-foot-deep pit in the hour it took us to track them down."

"I don't think the people who read dime novels worry about things like that."

"Perhaps not. I suppose we all look for different things in a story." Buckley pushed the manuscript across the desk towards Harlan. "And what ending to this story will you accept enough for you to leave me alone?"

"I guess you'll need to bring Frank Hunter to justice, find Fergal and Randolph's stolen exhibit, the missing Sergeant Woody, and also you'll need to track down those gun-runners."

"Is that all?" Buckley said then flinched and roved his gaze up to look over Harlan's shoulder.

Harlan turned to see Sergeant Dodge leaning in through the door.

"You have to come quickly," Emerson said in a low but urgent tone, "I've got some news on the gun-runners."

"You sure?" Buckley said, standing. "I thought that threat was all in your new major's mind."

"No, it's true, after all. We've just discovered that there's been a sneak raid on the fort. Five boxes of rifles have been stolen from the armory."

"Any clues as to who took them?" Buckley asked while rummaging in his desk for his gun.

"Yeah, luckily we have two witnesses who saw the gun-runners leaving—"

"Fergal O'Brien and Randolph McDougal, I presume" Buckley muttered. He thrust the gun in his holster.

Outside the fort gates Randolph knelt to peer intently at the ground and examine the numerous rutted wagon trails.

"So . . . ?" He broke off from asking Fergal his question to look around and check nobody was close enough to hear him.

Twenty yards away, Major Mulhoon and his soldiers were mounted up and bristling with almost as much weaponry as they were aiming to find. He and his troopers were waiting in a disciplined line, but behind them Marshal Buckley was striding away from the law office with Harlan hurrying behind.

Harlan was grinning, Buckley wasn't.

When Buckley reached them, leaving Harlan to stand beside the major, he stomped to a halt and loomed over Randolph, tapping a foot on the ground insistently.

"What are you doing?" Buckley demanded.

"Major Mulhoon has employed us as special cavalry envoys to help him catch these gun-runners."

"And do what? Cure his leather saddle with your tonic to give him a more comfortable ride?"

"No," Randolph said, standing. "He's employed us for our tracking skills."

"You two haven't got no tracking skills."

Randolph pouted with mock indignation.

"Just because that pursuit we staged for Harlan's benefit yesterday wasn't for real, it doesn't mean we can't track."

Buckley narrowed his eyes. "Which just brings up the question of whether or not *this* pursuit is for real."

From the corner of his eye Randolph noted that this comment had made Fergal fidget, but he was out of Buckley's view, so he kept his gaze stern.

"Major Mulhoon thinks it is. He says five hundred rifles were stolen from the fort and we just happened to be in the right place at the right time to see a wagon leaving town. We intend to follow its trail and help him reclaim those guns before they fall into the wrong hands. I thought you'd be pleased. We're helping to keep the peace in Fort Arlen, and you'll get the welcome bonus of giving your Marshal Blood devotee something else to write about."

Buckley glanced around and confirmed that Harlan had slipped in at the back of the troopers and so was out of earshot.

"There is nothing to be pleased about here. Two days ago I was sitting with my feet up in my office reading a Marshal Blood adventure, mildly irritated that the biggest problem I'd had to face all year was a spree of unsolved pig rustling. Then, within hours of you riding into town, I have more pig rustling, an apparent kidnapping and a raging gun battle, both not for real. Now I have gun-running. I can't help but make a connection."

Randolph put on an aggrieved expression, giving Fergal time to interject.

"Your suspicions are most unwelcome," he said. "So spell it out instead of insinuating."

"All right. I reckon you two have moved on from pig rustling to gun-running and I intend to prove it. Then you'll be looking at the inside of my jail cell for—"

"For slightly less time than you will." Fergal snorted a chuckle. "Because I just wonder how the townsfolk will react when they learn their town marshal helped stage a kidnapping and a gunfight just so he'd look good in a Marshal Blood adventure."

Buckley stabbed a firm finger against Fergal's chest.

"Are you blackmailing me?"

"I didn't say that, but I am saying we are all in this together. So the quicker we help Major Mulhoon find these stolen rifles, the quicker we'll meet Sergeant

Woody, the quicker we'll find our exhibit, the quicker Harlan will have his story, and the quicker you'll get back to reading about Marshal Blood."

Buckley opened his mouth to spout more threats but behind them impatience finally got the better of Major Mulhoon.

"You men," he shouted, "stop wasting time with all that talking. There are gun-runners out there who need shooting up."

With a last glare at both men, Buckley left them and headed to the back of the troopers to join Harlan, leaving Randolph to return to employing his tracking skills.

For long moments he stared down at the ground then resumed his interrupted conversation with Fergal.

"So," he said, "what exactly am I supposed to be looking for when I'm doing this here tracking?"

"Tracks, I presume," Fergal murmured.

Chapter Seven

"*I* have every faith in you," Marshal Blood said.

"Glad to hear it," Randolph McDougal said, still keeping his earnest gaze on the ground while he searched for the almost imperceptible spoor left by the gun-runners. "You can rely on me and my stalwart friend to help you complete your mission."

Randolph dismounted then knelt. When he sniffed a handful of earth, the cavalrymen joined Marshal Blood in looking at him with respect burning in their eyes.

"What are you looking for, man?" Major Mulhoon asked.

"An upturned stone, a crushed blade of grass, a trapped hair," Randolph said, his confident *tone hinting at his great wisdom, the sunlight illuminating his keen eyes.*

"I'm impressed," Mulhoon said. "Maybe when we've shot up the gun-runners, you can teach my men your craft."

"I could try," Randolph said lightly, "but I intend to leave town soon and my skills have taken me a lifetime to perfect."

Major Mulhoon nodded, accepting that the great skill Randolph possessed was beyond the learning of most men.

Randolph had already deduced the gun-runners had passed this way an hour ago merely by putting an ear to the ground. He had also decided that two men were on the wagon purely from the depth of the wheel ruts he'd found in town.

This latter revelation had impressed even his brave and resourceful companion, Fergal.

Major Mulhoon dismounted and joined Randolph.

"So tell me," he said with awe in his tone, "how exactly is wetting your finger and sticking it in the air telling you where these gun-runners are?"

Randolph McDougal wiped his finger on his jacket and faced up to the major.

"Please don't question my methods," he said. "I'll help you track them down as I promised."

"Without your *help* I could have found them myself

by now," Mulhoon said. "I know you were just following those wheel tracks we all saw in town until you lost them two miles back. I will not waste any more of my time watching you act the fool and lead me around in circles until you accidentally stumble across them again."

Randolph gulped. "I'm not doing that. I have a genuine skill, and from consideration of all the evidence I have deduced the gun-runners stopped not fifty yards from here."

Mulhoon slapped his hands on his hips. "And how did you deduce that?"

"Because the pattern of hoofprints I found earlier told me the horses were tired and needed a rest. Also the prevailing wind was from the south and the gun-runners were heading into that wind, but then the wind swung round, and . . ." Randolph licked his finger and raised it then slowly swung it round until it was pointing at a stretch of scrub beyond a stream, fifty yards ahead. "And because I can see the five crates of rifles over there."

Mulhoon did a double-take then swung round to follow the direction of Randolph's pointing. Sure enough, fifty yards ahead the missing five crates were sitting, half-buried in the scrub.

He acknowledged Randolph with a crisp salute then turned to his troopers.

"Draw your guns, men," he said, whipping out his revolver. "It's time to shoot 'em up."

Randolph just had enough time to dive for cover before the troopers lined up.

Mulhoon faced the crates, considering the quiet scene, then raised a hand.

"Is anyone over there by the crates?" he shouted. He waited for almost a whole second before lowering his hand and blasting lead at the crates.

After a few rounds, his troopers joined in and laid down a burst of gunfire at the crates and the surrounding area. Clumps of earth and splinters flew as the slugs cannoned around the crates.

With the troopers not being as trigger-happy as Mulhoon was, the gunfire rattled away in sporadic bursts for over two minutes, giving Mulhoon enough time to reload four times and to loose off enough lead to pepper the whole area.

Finally he gave the order to stop firing, even though he was the only one still blasting away.

Then, through the swirling gunsmoke, Mulhoon rode on to investigate. While Emerson caught Randolph's eye with a knowing and exasperated look, as for the first time Mulhoon justified his name and reputation, Fergal sidled over to join Randolph.

"Good tracking there, Randolph," he said, watching Mulhoon circle around the crates.

"I know," Randolph whispered, leaning towards him. "I thought for a while back there I'd have to do some real tracking. I couldn't remember where we'd left them."

"But at least we left them somewhere quiet. It doesn't pay to be standing in front of the major when he's on the trail of gun-runners." Fergal shrugged. "But not to worry. This should all be over soon. The rifles will be back in the fort, we can find Frank Hunter and our missing treasure, and Harlan will have his story."

Randolph watched Mulhoon dismount and stalk around the crates, loosing off the occasional shot at anything that moved such as the grass swaying in the wind. Then, after planting another round into each of the crates, he whipped off the first lid to peer inside.

With his mouth falling open in what appeared to be surprise, he then tore off the second and third lids.

"I still don't see how this gun-running will get rid of him," Randolph said.

"Because amongst the major's many faults, he's also a man of duty. He's sure to file a report to his superiors that while he was in command someone broke into the fort and stole five hundred rifles. The military take a dim view of that sort of thing. I reckon a demotion will be heading his way before long."

Randolph nodded, but before he could reply, Mulhoon thrust his revolver back in its holster and signaled for everyone to approach with a short, irritated gesture. Randolph set off while Mulhoon levered off the lids of the final crates, but long before he reached him he could see what had irritated Mulhoon.

The crates were empty.

Someone had stolen the stolen rifles.

While Major Mulhoon debated his next actions with Sergeant Emerson, his finger pointing and significant looks at his gun suggesting those actions would involve him finding someone to shoot real quick, Fergal drew Randolph away.

"Are you sure you left them here?" he whispered.

"You were with me," Randolph said. "You saw me hide them in the scrub."

"I know. I was just hoping you might have come back or something . . ."

"Stop looking for a way out of this. There really are gun-runners about and we delivered five crates of rifles to them."

"And nobody must ever find that out," Fergal said, backing away slowly towards his horse. "We'll just stay out of this from now on and let the major shoot whoever he likes."

"Provided Marshal Buckley doesn't arrest us first," Randolph said, drawing Fergal's attention to the advancing and glowering lawman. But when Buckley reached them he walked straight on by to join Major Mulhoon.

"What's your plan, Major?" he asked.

Mulhoon finished relaying an order to Emerson with a quick slap of his revolver and a firm salute then turned to him.

"It's simple," he said. "I will track down the gun-runners and give them a taste of hot lead."

Buckley winced. "Then I'd be obliged if we could work together on this."

"Oh?" Mulhoon said, taking a long pace to stand before Buckley. He found they were on the same eye-line, but to give himself an advantage he raised his heels. "Go on."

"First," Buckley said, gesturing towards Fergal and Randolph, "don't waste your time getting those idiots' *help* to track the missing rifles."

"Agreed," Mulhoon said, his voice catching, as if he seldom uttered that word.

"Second, keep those guns holstered. This is a quiet town and I—"

"If that's your second, I hope for your sake there isn't a third."

"There is. I will take charge of this investigation. As the legally sworn–in—"

"You will not!" Mulhoon roared, the force of his anger making Buckley back away a pace. "This investigation is a serious matter and that calls for swift, military action. A lawman who can't even round up pig rustlers knows nothing about swift action."

Buckley gulped, then glanced over towards Harlan to see if he'd heard this rebuke, but Harlan was sitting, frantically scribbling down his version of the recent events and not paying this confrontation any attention.

When Buckley turned back he didn't get the chance

to deliver a retort as Mulhoon had already turned away from him and resumed ordering Emerson about.

Buckley glared at Mulhoon's back while rocking back and forth on his heels, but then his fighting spirit eroded away. His shoulders slumped and he turned away.

Fergal stood to the side to intercept him and provided a consoling smile.

"Don't worry about Mulhoon's swift, military action," he said. "He's a fool. The only thing he's shot up so far is five empty crates."

Buckley glanced at his hands, which were shaking.

"I don't care what he does next because he was right. I'm not the man for any kind of action, swift and military or any other kind. I can't even catch—" Buckley brightened, as if a sudden pleasing thought had come to mind, then looked up at Fergal. "But if I'm not getting involved in the search for the gun-runners, that means I'm free to consider you two again."

"Don't go no further with that threat. You can't change the wording of our agreement."

"I can when our deal was that you'd give Harlan what he wanted so that he'd move on and leave me alone. Except he's still here, scribbling away about my life, which I'm not exactly enjoying right now, while back in the law office I've got an empty cell just waiting to be filled with a couple of pig rustlers."

Buckley cast a significant look at Fergal that promised they'd speak later, and not on friendly terms, then headed off to join Harlan. A brief discussion ensued after which they mounted up and headed back towards Fort Arlen, leaving Fergal and Randolph with the cavalrymen.

For the next five minutes they waited to confirm that Mulhoon didn't want their help again, while debating which excuses they'd offer if he did. But when Mulhoon had seen everything he wanted to see here, he ordered his men to move on out with only a brief sneering glance their way.

Emerson slipped in at the back of the line of riders and followed them, but when the group were fifty yards on, he slowed to let them get ahead then doubled back.

"Everything appears to be going well," he said when he joined them.

"I'm pleased," Fergal said with genuine relief in his tone. "I thought you might be worried that this has got out of control."

"I have no idea what you mean and neither do I have any idea how those rifles came to be out here." Emerson looked ahead at the receding riders with his jaw set firm.

"Of course you don't, and I'll be sure to repeat that if anyone ever asks me."

"Now that we've made that clear . . ." Emerson leaned down from the saddle and despite the fact nobody else was nearby, he lowered his voice. "Yeah, it sure is sad those rifles have fallen into the wrong hands, but that ain't as important as how this'll look on the major's record. The rifles going missing for a few hours was bad enough, but having them stolen from his fort permanently is disastrous. I reckon he's sure to be replaced within days."

"And then you'll tell us where Sergeant Woody is?"

"Sure will." Emerson saluted in a fairly efficient manner for him then hurried after the other riders.

"So that went well, after all," Randolph said as they walked to their horses. "Just a pity it never occurred to us that the rifles going missing permanently would be such good news or we could have hidden them somewhere where the major would never find them."

Fergal considered the departing sergeant.

"Yeah, it sure is odd that *we* didn't think of doing that."

Chapter Eight

"*The* rifles are gone!" Major Mulhoon spat out.

"*Do not despair, my noble friend,*" Marshal Blood said, "*I'll find 'em, or my middle name isn't Trouble.*"

"*You won't. This is a military matter. I'll be the one who finds the men responsible or my middle name isn't worth mentioning.*"

"*Why, what is it?*"

"*Timothy.*"

Marshal Blood firmed his jaw, then reluctantly tipped his hat.

"*Then I'll leave you, Timothy. I have a stolen exhibit to track down and a swine by the name of Frank Hunter to root out.*"

"So," Randolph McDougal said, idly spinning a jeweled circle on the lid of their casket, "how will we ever find our stolen exhibit?"

Fergal joined him in sitting on the back of the wagon.

"As long as nobody does any searching in here, I reckon we might be able to find it."

Randolph looked out of the back of the wagon, taking in Fort Arlen's main road then the fort and beyond.

"After an appropriately long search."

Fergal cringed. "I don't fancy searching all over looking for something that's sitting in the back of our wagon."

"Me neither, but to keep Marshal Buckley on our side we have to keep Harlan happy." Randolph lowered his voice as he mentioned the issue that had increasingly plagued him during the four days since they'd taken the rifles from the armory. "And if we were to wander around, looking as if we're searching for the missing treasure, we could also put that time to good use and look for the stolen rifles."

"Why?" Fergal spluttered, aghast.

"Because we were the ones who stole them in the first place."

Fergal winced and darted his gaze around as if he feared someone might be close enough to overhear them.

"Never say that again," he whispered, "even when

we are alone. We didn't steal them. We *borrowed* them with Emerson's help. We weren't to know someone would then come along and steal them."

"We weren't, but it did happen and that means we are responsible."

Fergal sighed and placed a consoling hand on Randolph's shoulder.

"You have a good heart, Randolph, but if whoever stole them is that dangerous, they'd have probably stolen them from the fort anyhow. It wasn't that difficult, was it?"

"I guess it wasn't, but it sure is hard to find them. Even a disciplined man like Major Mulhoon is getting nowhere."

Fergal snorted, shaking his head. "Perhaps if he stopped shooting up the countryside for a few minutes, he might give himself time to think."

Randolph nodded. Like everyone in town, they'd judged how the search was progressing from the sound of distant gunfire.

"Hopefully he'll run out of bullets before someone gets hurt."

"Which brings up the fact that our motive in borrowing those rifles was honorable. We just wanted to get rid of the major."

"You have an odd interpretation of honor." Randolph lowered his head, accepting he'd never talk Fergal round to his way of thinking when he was this determined. "How long do you reckon it'll be before the bad news about those stolen rifles gets him moved on?"

"It shouldn't be too much longer. There's been plenty of activity going on down by the telegraph office over this and some new cavalry officers rode into the fort the other morning."

"How do you know they were new?"

"Because they were smartly dressed, keen-eyed and straight-backed." Fergal looked down the road and narrowed his eyes. "And I reckon they might be coming out of the fort now."

Randolph slipped out the back of the wagon to look towards the fort and saw that Fergal was right. A cortege of officers was coming through the gates. He looked for Major Mulhoon, hoping he might be being taken away to face punishment, but he wasn't amongst the group.

With much shouting the men formed into a line then headed towards town at a gallop. When they reached the main road, one rider peeled off from the group and swung in to ride towards the law office. Then, without breaking his horse's stride, he leaned out from the saddle, yanked a poster from his jacket and slapped it on the wall.

The poster stuck, but the rider didn't even look back to check that it had as he carried on to rejoin his companions in hurtling out of town on whatever mission they were on.

"Now that sure was quick to get a poster printed up," Randolph said, setting off to see what it said.

"That's the military for you," Fergal said. "Quick and efficient."

"And dangerous," Randolph said when he saw the bold writing proclaiming an offer that was clear enough.

"One thousand dollars reward," Fergal said, reading, "for information leading to the recovery of five crates of rifles stolen from Fort Arlen and to the arrest of the people responsible."

"I told you this was serious."

"I know," Fergal said, grinning, "one thousand dollars. That sure is an enticing offer. I'm almost tempted to hand ourselves in and claim that reward."

"But not tempted enough to try to find the rifles?"

"Of course not. That many rifles is sure to lead to shooting, and not just from the major." Fergal turned to go, then shrieked and backed into Randolph, who turned to see that Sergeant Emerson Dodge had arrived unannounced.

"I see that reward poster has interested you," he said.

"Only slightly," Fergal said cautiously.

"You will be more than be slightly interested," Emerson said, advancing on Fergal and forcing him to back away until he walked into the wall. "You will try to earn that reward."

"Why?"

"Because your plan to get rid of the major has not only failed, it's backfired so badly the fort now has ten more officers just like him."

"Those men who just rode out of town?"

Emerson loomed over Fergal and waved his arms in exasperation.

"Sure. Major Mulhoon convinced his superiors that the rifles getting stolen wasn't his fault, seeing as how Sergeant Woody was in charge of the armory and how he suspects him of being the gun-runners' ringleader. So they've sent him ten regulars to help him track them down, all graduates from West Point, all keen and peppered up with military discipline, and all just as trigger-happy as the major is."

Fergal offered a tentative smile. "Then perhaps they'll be keen enough to find the gun-runners quickly and get things back to normal."

"They sure won't find anything," Emerson spluttered.

"Why not?"

Emerson opened his mouth then snapped it shut as if he'd decided not to give his original retort.

"In my experience those military types just ride around, enjoying themselves shooting up anything that moves, while the rest of us polish the stockade. Life won't ever get back to normal, unless I sort this out, and the only thing I can think of doing right now is to find those gun-runners." Emerson gave Fergal then Randolph a significant look.

"Don't waste your breath with that threat," Randolph said, pacing up to Emerson and giving Fergal a chance to slip away from the wall. "We took the rifles from the armory with your help."

Emerson turned his annoyed gaze on to Randolph.

"You did not get my help. I only let you into the fort to discuss legitimate business. I was completely unaware of what you then did while you were inside. I will be horrified if I ever discover you had anything to do with the gun-running."

Fergal snorted with irritation. "You knew *exactly* what we were doing."

Emerson sneered. "Perhaps I did, but after Randolph's pathetic tracking performance, the major already trusts you less than he trusts most people. So whose word will the major, a man whose personal idol is Lieutenant Colonel George Custer, choose to believe? Mine, or the people who own a report written by his hero about the battle in which he died?"

"I accept your point," Fergal murmured, his tone low and urgent, "but I also suspect Major Mulhoon isn't enthused by your military performance. He's sure to investigate you and I wonder what he'll find?"

The two men locked gazes, each man searching the other man's eyes to see who was bluffing. Neither man looked away, but Emerson was the first to speak.

"Take this as a threat if you want, Fergal, but there's only one way this can ever end. Get rid of the major and those other West Point officers. Do it by getting him suspended or finding those rifles or whatever it is you have to do, but get him out of my fort. Because if you don't, not only will you never get to meet Sergeant Woody, I will turn you both in and claim that reward for myself."

Chapter Nine

*M*arshal Blood kicked open the door to the shack, his gun already drawn and cocked. Inside, three men sat hunched around a table, a game of poker in progress.

"I've come for Frank Hunter," the lawman said, stepping inside.

At the mention of this name, hands strayed towards holsters.

"Frank Hunter's a pig," one man said, eyeing the marshal with surly disinterest.

"So I've heard. But I've got a nice warm pig-pen back in the law office just waiting to be filled by his ugly hide."

"Just leave us alone, Marshal Blood." The

man glanced down at his holster. "We're not talking to no lawman."

Marshal Blood chuckled, his laughter as hollow as an open grave, then firmed his gun hand.

"I'd hoped you'd say that."

Harlan Finchley glared through the window of his hotel room to look down on the road below, irritated by his story's lack of progress.

He knew he was being impatient in expecting Marshal Buckley's investigation to proceed quickly, but after the initial excitement of the raging gun battle followed by the gun-runners' daring raid on the fort, events had stagnated.

Worse, there was no sign of anything changing.

He mooched around his room, but he couldn't find anything to occupy his mind.

So he decided that as it'd been several hours since he'd last seen Marshal Buckley, it would be all right for him to get an update. He set off for the law office, but this time he was too pessimistic about the possibility of receiving any news to bother bringing his manuscript.

When he arrived, Buckley had his feet on his desk reading then did a double-take and shoved what appeared from his quick sighting to be an orange-covered book into his drawer.

"You reading a dime novel?" Harlan asked.

"Of course not. I was reviewing witness reports."

"About the stolen treasure?" He watched Buckley shake his head. "Then Frank Hunter, the missing Sergeant Woody, the gun—?"

"No." Buckley banged a fist on his desk then looked aloft, taking deep breaths. "On the pig rustling."

Harlan knew he was annoying his idol with his constant questions but he didn't see he had a choice.

Coming here didn't move the investigation on, but neither did staying in his hotel room as Buckley had requested. At least coming here gave him a chance to talk with the marshal and perhaps learn something more about the man and his activities, even if the only thing the lawman wanted to talk about was pig rustling.

"That mean you've got a new lead?" Harlan asked, trying to gather some enthusiasm at the thought of something happening, even if it involved the most mundane matter.

"None yet," Buckley said, his tone calming down, "which in itself is interesting. Pigs were going missing almost daily for three months, but then all the pig rustling stopped this week."

Harlan nodded encouragingly, but when Buckley added nothing more, he sighed in exasperation.

"How can you bother about something like that when you have so much more to consider?"

"A lawman's duty never ends, Harlan," Buckley said with the weary tone of someone who'd already answered several variations of that question, "whether the crime be minor or large."

Buckley chastised him some more, but he didn't provide any more information beyond his initial comment before he shooed him out the office to let him get back to his important business.

Once outside Harlan stomped to a standstill in the road. He looked up at his hotel room. The thought of sitting up there with only a blank sheet of paper for company didn't enthuse him.

Buckley's increasingly brusque manner had also aggrieved him, and the few sketchy details he had provided would give him only a few more sentences. Unless . . .

Five minutes later he was riding out of town on the horse Buckley had lent him earlier, to begin investigating on his own.

He kept to the trail heading east until ten miles out of town he located the dugout Fergal and Randolph had visited on their way to town. He found Christopher, the farmer Buckley had told him about, in surprisingly good spirits.

"Come on in," Christopher said beckoning him into his house. "I'm always pleased to introduce passersby to my family."

Harlan lowered his head to enter Christopher's dugout and found that Christopher's family wasn't what he'd expected. Christopher was the only human member of the household, not that there'd be room for anyone else as the pigpens took up most of the single room.

As they exchanged pleasantries, the pigs bustled

around and looked up at Harlan with eager interest in their small eyes.

"Your pigs all look fine," Harlan said with what he hoped was the right amount of interest and approval in his tone.

"They sure are. I was really worried about one of my little ones, but he'll be fine thanks to that miracle worker Fergal O'Brien."

Harlan nodded. "He and Randolph are fine men."

"Two fine men indeed. I was skeptical at first, thinking them cheap hucksters, and when my little ones tasted their medicine and ran amok I was sure. But then they settled down, came back home, and since then they've never been healthier."

Harlan had already gathered that Christopher thought more highly of his pigs than any person, so he lowered his voice to a suitably somber tone.

"I did hear about your one tragedy though." Harlan waited, but Christopher just shook his head. "I mean the little . . . big one that got blasted to . . . came to an unfortunate end."

Christopher furrowed his brow. "None of them met with an unfortunate end. They ran away and at first I was worried, but they all came back."

"But a hog ran amok in the fort."

Christopher shrugged. "A hog might have done, but it wasn't one of mine. My family did a bit of roaming but now everyone is back where they should be, at home."

"That sure is intriguing," Harlan murmured, mostly to himself as an idea stirred in his mind.

He'd spent the last few days trying to get inside Marshal Buckley's mind so that he could write about him. Now for the first time the effort was paying dividends as he found he was starting to think like a lawman.

Then he noticed that Christopher was looking at him oddly and he realized he'd been silent for a while. So he bade him and his family good-bye and headed off back to Fort Arlen.

This time he rode along in a more optimistic frame of mind as new and interesting thoughts vied for his attention.

Maybe, he wondered, the pig rustling was connected to the missing treasure and the gun-running, after all, even if he couldn't see how just yet . . .

"Stop trying to look like a tracker," Fergal said, looking down from his horse at the crouching Randolph. "You didn't fool Major Mulhoon and you sure won't fool me. We've lost the trail and you won't ever find it again."

Randolph straightened from his studious consideration of the ground.

"I wasn't trying to fool you. Those trackers have to be looking for something when they look at the ground, and I'm sure if I look for long enough I'll see what it is."

Fergal snorted. "Try licking your finger. That worked the last time."

Randolph laughed. "Anything works when you can see the crates, but how difficult can this be?"

"Too difficult for us. If the major couldn't find any trails to follow, I doubt we will." Fergal glanced back towards the location of the crates, a mile behind them.

They had searched in many places, but they'd always returned to the crates, assuming that following the trail that they could see heading away from them represented their best chance of success. But this was the furthest they'd been able to go while still being able to see a trail, although they were unsure whether the one they'd found was the right one.

"We've only spent two days on this search."

"I prefer to say we've *wasted* two days and we've learnt nothing, no clues as to where the rifles went, no gun-runners, nothing."

"Failure shouldn't stop us trying," Randolph said, mounting his horse.

"I wish something would." Fergal sighed. "But I guess if we're still going to waste our time, we need to double back and see if we can pick up the trail again."

"Or maybe we could ask Major Mulhoon for some ideas." Randolph pointed, drawing Fergal's attention to a group of approaching troopers.

"Can't see how that'll help. He's found nothing either, even with his West Point officers."

"Then we can ask him where he's looked, then go somewhere else."

"We can tell where he's looked without his help," Fergal murmured. "We just have to find the places that don't have any bullet holes."

Randolph snorted a rueful laugh. Then they settled down to await Major Mulhoon. He was riding with a group of the original troopers, who were lagging behind him, riding hunched up and weary in the saddle. Mulhoon was showing no such strain as he drew up before them and considered them with stiff-backed authority.

"Howdy," Fergal said. "You having any luck with your search?"

"We weren't," Mulhoon said, eyeing both men. "But I'm feeling more confident now."

"Why?" Fergal asked, with a quaver in his voice.

"Because I have a very good question to ask you."

Randolph saw Mulhoon's hand drift towards his revolver and so he shot Fergal a significant glance, silently reminding him of Mulhoon's reputation as a man who only asked questions to distract you while he shot you.

Fergal returned that glance then darted his eyes to the side, conveying a course of action quietly in a way that only people who had known each other for years could.

"I'm sure that question will be an interesting one, but first I have an observation to make." Fergal pointed over Mulhoon's shoulder then raised his voice. "I can see the gun-runners hiding over there."

"Where?" Mulhoon shouted, drawing his revolver and turning at the hip to look around. He stared in the direction of Fergal's pointing while the other troopers dragged their horses round to look, but the plains behind them were deserted.

By the time he'd loosed off a few rounds of exploratory gunfire then turned back, the plains before him were deserted too, or at least they would be as soon as Fergal and Randolph had made good their escape.

"Get 'em, men!" Mulhoon shouted, spurring his horse into pursuit.

A hundred yards ahead, Randolph glanced back to see Mulhoon and the troopers after them, then turned to the front.

"The gun-runners are hiding over there," he intoned, shaking his head. "Is that the best you could do?"

"Quit complaining," Fergal shouted. "It worked!"

Randolph provided a noncommittal grunt as gunfire whined from behind them, although where it landed he couldn't tell.

"But not well enough. Shoot-em-up is about to show us how he got his name."

Fergal nodded, then both men settled down to hard riding as behind them Mulhoon closed on them, punctuating each advance with another gunshot.

The abandoned crates were a quarter-mile ahead, which meant they were still eight miles out of town, when for the first time Randolph heard a bullet whistle past his shoulder. Fergal also heard it and darted a glance at Randolph.

"We're not going to get away," he shouted. "We need to make a stand. Ahead at the crates will do."

Randolph had never known Fergal to make a stand before and he presumed what he really meant was he would hide in a crate while Randolph made a stand, but Randolph didn't see they had any other options. So when they reached the crates, they dragged their horses to a halt and leaped down.

As expected Fergal moved to climb in a crate, but then screeched and stumbled back a pace. A moment later a trooper emerged from the crate.

"Trap!" Randolph shouted.

He swirled round, but it was only to see more troopers stand up all around him. Every one of them had a gun trained on him, and worse, they were all the new officers.

Seeing no other option, Randolph raised his arms. A few moments later, Major Mulhoon arrived. He drew his horse to a halt and stared down at them as his hand moved to his holster, but before he could act, Fergal spoke up.

"I'm glad you arrived," he said, smiling with more confidence than he should show in this situation. "I assume you have our money."

"What money?" Mulhoon demanded.

"Our reward for finding the gun-runners." Fergal glanced at his jacket and getting his meaning, Mulhoon nodded, letting Fergal reach inside and withdraw the reward poster. "One thousand dollars it says here."

"That mean you've found them?" Mulhoon said, narrowing his eyes.

"Not exactly, but we were the only ones who saw them leaving town and without our help you'd have never found these crates. I reckon that should be worth something."

"That information was so worthless it gets what it deserves—nothing!"

"That's a pity. In that case we'd better get back to our search and see if we can earn that thousand dollars in a way that will satisfy you."

Fergal moved to leave, but the nearest trooper lunged forward and slapped a hand on his shoulder.

"You are going nowhere," he grunted, "until Major Mulhoon says so."

Fergal looked up at Mulhoon and raised his voice to provide a fair impression of Mulhoon's strident tones.

"Then let us go, sir! We haven't got all day to stand around when there's gun-runners to shoot up."

"We haven't," Mulhoon said, all but standing to attention in the saddle. He looked around at his men, then gestured overhead. "Move on out, men. We have a mission to complete."

Randolph kept quiet and didn't move as the troopers emerged from their crates and headed into the scrub to collect their horses. But Fergal showed no such caution as he paraded around, looking everyone up and down as if he were inspecting them until Mulhoon led the troopers off.

Fergal watched them until he was sure they wouldn't turn back then put a hand to his heart and flopped down to sit on the ground.

"How did you do that?" Randolph said with genuine admiration. "I was sure Mulhoon was all set to deal with us as if we were the gun-runners."

Fergal took deep breaths to calm himself. "If there's one thing you can rely on, it's the military mindset. Military men like military discipline and that means they'll always respond to military bluster. I just gave him what he's used to and so doubt never entered his mind."

"I'm impressed. Hopefully the next time we meet Major Mulhoon he won't have found the time to think and let doubt enter that military mind."

"But whether he starts doubting or not, we should head back to Fort Arlen now. I reckon we've been going about this search the wrong way." Fergal gestured at their horses then the crates. "Riding around chasing after rifles and gun-runners isn't the usual way we do things."

"Getting chased is," Randolph said ruefully then

joined him in sitting on the ground. "What do you suggest?"

"I don't know, but I do know we've not been thinking properly. Sergeant Dodge let us break into the fort to steal those rifles. He's not exactly a dedicated military man but that's mighty odd."

"And he didn't appear to be particularly upset or surprised when we discovered the rifles were missing."

"Exactly, Randolph. It was almost as if he expected them to be taken. And did you notice what he said when he threatened us outside the law office?"

Randolph cast his mind back, then shook his head. "No."

"When I said those new West Point officers would be sure to find the guns, he said they would never be able to do that, then covered himself with an excuse."

Randolph narrowed his eyes. "You saying he set us up? That he helped someone steal them after we'd removed them from the fort, the riskiest part of the endeavor?"

"I'm not sure yet," Fergal said, shrugging.

He stood and beckoned for Randolph to follow him to the nearest crate. Slowly he wandered around it, murmuring to himself and looking at the crate from all angles.

"What are you looking for?"

"I don't know . . ." Fergal peered inside then jerked up grinning. "Come and see this, Randolph."

Randolph peered over his shoulder, then shook his head.

"Sorry, Fergal, I don't see nothing but an empty crate."

"You don't see nothing. So what else don't you see?"

Randolph furrowed his brow, but Fergal grunted, encouraging him to answer.

"I don't know what you mean. All I can see is that there aren't no rifles in there."

"You're right, but it's not just the absence of rifles that's interesting. I'm talking about an absence beyond the mere absence of what you'd expect to see in a crate marked up as containing one hundred rifles."

"You've confused me there, Fergal."

Fergal uttered a long sigh, as if Randolph should have already understood his meaning.

"Then if you won't use your eyes and your mind, use your other senses." Fergal reached down into the crate and swept his hand along the bottom, coating his fingers with a fine white powder. "Scrape some of that up then lick your fingers."

Randolph balked but he'd had to consume worse things while selling the universal remedy, so he scraped his fingers along the bottom then dabbed his tongue to the powder.

"Salt."

"It is. Have you ever known salt to get packed into a crate full of rifles?"

"I guess not."

"And do you know what a hundred rifles smell like?"

"Not really."

"Well, think about what you reckon they should smell like then put your head in the crate and sniff."

Randolph formed an image in his mind of a gun and its smell then ducked his head into the crate and dragged in a long breath through his nostrils. He flinched back up, his stomach churning at the rank odor.

"That sure isn't no rifle smell," he said, turning away to cough and splutter.

"It isn't. But what does it smell like?"

Randolph pondered, trying to place the odor. Then, on seeing several flies buzzing around, he nodded.

"It smells like meat." Randolph batted the salt from his fingers. "Yeah, meat that's gone bad after being left out in the sun for days."

"It is meat," Fergal said, smiling. "Or to be more precise, pork."

Chapter Ten

"*So* Frank Hunter is working for Major Mulhoon?" Randolph McDougal said.

"Not exactly," Marshal Blood said, completing the story he'd uncovered. "Mulhoon has his own agenda, but if in his determination to find the gun-runners he has to ignore Frank's activities, he will."

"How did you find all that out?"

Blood glanced at his gun, then twirled it back into his holster.

"Sometimes a man sleeps easier if he don't ask too many questions."

"Then," Fergal O'Brien said, "we'll deal with it. Frank Hunter has our treasure, but if we can *lead him to believe that we can open it, that could draw him out of hiding."*

"Fergal," the marshal urged, clasping his wiry arm, "my dear and trusted friend, that's a fine plan, but you must let the law deal with this. I can't let you risk your life over this."

Fergal ground his firm jaw, suggesting he would refuse the lawman's demand, but then nodded.

"All right, Marshal Blood. I trust your judgement."

"As I do yours."

With his approval ringing in their ears, Fergal and Randolph left the law office, but the moment the door closed, Marshal Blood checked his six-shooter then hurried to the door.

He watched the two men stride away down the road and when he was certain they were too far away to see him, he slipped outside, planning to follow them and find out where they went.

He trusted these brave men, but sometimes you had to save your friends from themselves . . .

"Obliged for the information, Harlan," Marshal Ed Buckley said, letting genuine respect creep into his voice, something he hadn't provided for several days.

Harlan smiled. "That mean you don't mind if I come to see you again?"

Although Harlan's evidence had interested him, Buckley was still tempted to refuse his request and finally end his unwelcome attention, but after a moment's thought he provided a reluctant nod.

"Sure, I guess."

"I'll see you later, then," Harlan said, hurrying for the door.

"Just make sure it is *later*," Buckley said without much hope, but Harlan didn't acknowledge him as he ran through the door and hurried across the road to his hotel. "Much, much later."

He sighed, pondering on what Harlan's information meant.

He didn't reach a firm decision, but for the first time in days he felt no urge to pull out his hastily tucked away Marshal Blood dime novel. Instead, he spread the recent reports and witness statements about the spree of pig rustling over his desk.

He read them, now convinced he was close to solving the case. Somewhere amongst the mass of statements would be the answer, and it had to involve Fergal and Randolph.

Almost every day for three months a pig had been stolen. Two consecutive days had never passed without another incident, but then last week it had all stopped, and on the very day Fergal and Randolph had ridden into town.

He had thought the fact that one of the hogs they'd given a tonic to had ended up in the fort, which they'd then visited, was conclusive proof of their guilt. Harlan's evidence appeared to disprove this theory, but as he considered the statements, in a curious way he decided Harlan's discovery provided even more definitive proof.

If there was one thing he'd learned about the tonic sellers, it was that they were devious, and slipping up so badly as to let a hog escape wasn't like them.

As he read, a new theory formed in his mind.

For the last three months they'd been out of town and behind the pig rustling. Then they'd grown in confidence and moved on to gun-running. They'd encouraged a previously stolen hog to run wild in the fort to give them a ruse to get to the armory and steal the rifles. Afterward they'd provided a distraction by offering their help, although that *help* only led Major Mulhoon to the empty crates.

To Buckley's way of thinking, the key to proving their guilt lay in answering the one unanswered question Harlan's new evidence had thrown up— where did the hog in the fort come from?

Buckley chided himself for agreeing with Sergeant Emerson Dodge's plan to eat the hog and so making it harder to find someone who might recognize the carcass. Then he remembered the wanted poster he'd torn down when Harlan had arrived.

Suddenly, he made the connection.

The hog in the poster had been seen roaming around some months ago, and it had had a distinctive pattern of markings on its face, markings that he now realized matched those on the dead hog in the fort. Intrigued now, he reached for, then straightened out, the poster.

Then he began reading.

Somewhere amongst the mass of statements there had to be one that'd tell him who had owned such a distinctive hog.

As he read, Buckley chuckled to himself, confident now that it was only a matter of time before he had Fergal and Randolph behind bars.

When Fergal and Randolph left the law office to head down the road to the fort, Fergal had such a spring in his step he was almost skipping.

"My universal remedy actually worked."

"On pigs," Randolph murmured. "But the more important fact is Marshal Buckley has still got it into his head we're behind the pig rustling going on around here."

"Forget that suspicious lawman and his ridiculous claims. I cured a pig."

"You did," Randolph said with the resigned air of a man who knew he'd be reminded of this repeatedly, or at least until after someone didn't fare so well after taking the tonic and Randolph could remind Fergal of that. "But what I don't understand is why Buckley enjoyed telling us that."

Randolph glanced back into the law office, seeing

that after telling them he would prove they were pig rustlers if it was the last thing he did, Marshal Buckley had hunched over his desk, presumably reading his Marshal Blood adventure.

"Buckley doesn't exactly get much excitement in Fort Arlen. That's probably the most investigating he's ever done." Fergal chuckled to himself. "A pig, I cured a sick pig!"

Randolph searched for something to say that would distract Fergal from continuing to mention this, then gave up and looked ahead to the fort.

With the increased tension in the town, two guards were on duty and this time they told them to remain outside as they got word to Emerson. When Emerson arrived he ordered the guards to let them enter and slowly they walked across the square.

"I heard about your encounter with Major Mulhoon," Emerson said. "He's impressed that you're the only people who are rising to the challenge of getting that reward."

"Let's hope he stays impressed."

"And why should you be interested in his approval? You're supposed to be removing him."

"We will, but it's always a good idea to have a man like him on your side, especially as I now have sufficient proof about the gun-runners to take to him." Fergal looked Emerson up and down.

"If that's you calling my bluff," Emerson snapped, halting in the middle of the square, "then I call it back.

Major Mulhoon will return soon and I'm prepared to tell him everything I know."

"But will you? And what will you tell him? And will your explanation include details of how you helped us take five crates out of the fort?"

"You can't prove I did that," Emerson said, shaking his head, "but I can find witnesses who saw you leaving town at speed towards the place where we found the crates. Mulhoon's suspicious nature and a night spent on the receiving end of his questioning will fill in the rest."

"Except no matter how well he interrogates us and no matter how little he believes of our story that you were behind it, he won't be able to prove anything. Not without locating the rifles and rounding up the rest of the gun-runners, and we both know he can never do that, don't we?"

"He'll find them eventually. He's getting help now from those West Point officers. They can find anything and anyone."

Fergal snorted, then looked for support from Randolph, who provided his own prolonged snort. Then he locked gazes with Emerson and even from several yards away Randolph noticed the flickering in Emerson's gaze that said that for the first he was worried they understood his true purpose.

Fergal laughed, reducing the tension a little.

"You may be right. Like I guess happened at his last assignment, when Major Mulhoon searches for trouble he'll find it, even if he has to harass every innocent person in the county. But even if he finds a few rifles and can convince himself they are part of a larger conspiracy, will they actually be the rifles from this fort?"

"How can I possibly answer that?"

"I thought you might." Fergal looked around the square to confirm nobody was close enough to hear them. "Bearing in mind no rifles are actually missing."

Emerson gulped. "Five crates are missing."

"Five crates *are* missing. The trouble is none of them contained rifles."

"That's ridiculous." Emerson gestured at Randolph. "He dragged them out of the armory. He knows they were full of rifles."

"They were fairly heavy," Randolph said, "so there was something in them."

"But it wasn't rifles." Fergal walked back and forth twice to prolong the moment before he delivered the revelation he'd been looking forward to stating. "Here's the way it is—all that was in those crates was a consignment of stolen pork. The pig rustlers Marshal Buckley has been looking for are all troopers from this fort and unbeknown to Major Mulhoon he isn't chasing after gun-runners but pork-runners."

"Prove it."

"I might be able to, but why should I when we both know this is the truth? And it's a truth the major will uncover when he eventually comes across the leader of the pork-runners."

Emerson firmed his jaw as if he wouldn't retort but then with a sigh he let his shoulders slump.

"Sergeant Woody," he murmured, kicking at the dirt.

"That's the man." Fergal continued to glare at Emerson, but then softened his expression. "So I suggest now is the time for you to stop playing games with us and tell us where Woody is hiding."

"Why should I?"

"Because only then will be able to work out how we can get ourselves out of this mess before the trigger-happy Major Mulhoon works it all out for himself and comes looking for us."

Chapter Eleven

"*M*any years ago," *Fergal O'Brien announced, his eyes lively as he related the legend to his enraptured audience outside Fort Arlen's gates, "there was a young man who would one day become known as Saint Woody."*

"There's a saint called Woody?" someone asked.

"There sure is, and everyone knew him to be a valiant young man. One fine day he was tending his pigs, but he had become bored. He didn't want to be a pig farmer all his life and so he began to dream of achieving great things with—"

"Looking after pigs is a great thing," an aggrieved audience member muttered.

*"It is, but he dreamed of even greater things—
if that's possible—and as he dreamed, he looked
skyward. The clouds parted, thunder roared and
a vision came to him of a bewitching woman.
She glowed from head to foot and had a face that
shone with divine wisdom. With a beguiling toss
of her hair, she enticed Woody to join her in her
mountain lair."*

*"Did he go?" Major Mulhoon asked, step-
ping out through the gates to join the throng.*

*"He sure did. He left his pigs . . ."—Fergal
coughed—"after ensuring, of course, that they
were in safe hands, and trudged ever higher into
the hills. After many days, he reached the top of
a craggy mountain where the snow lay crisply on
the ground and the air was so thin it made him
gasp. There, he found a fabulous jeweled casket
and in that casket was the most stupendous treasure in all the world."*

"What was that treasure?" Mulhoon asked.

*"I don't know, because the bewitching woman
appeared to him again and beckoned Woody to
come closer and, just as he reached for the
treasure, she closed the lid of the fabulous casket."*

*Fergal paused and the dramatic interlude had
the desired effect when everyone edged forward
a pace and urged him to continue.*

"Then," Fergal said, "she asked Woody to

place the symbols on the lid in an order that would tell the story of his life, proclaiming that only that order would open the casket. Woody did this then left the mountain lair with her to roam the world, spreading a message of peace. When his family came looking for him, all they found was the casket and, when they tried to open it, they could not . . ."

"Because they didn't know the story of Woody's life?" Mulhoon asked.

"You've understood. Only Woody knew his own story, but if anyone should ever deduce it, he can turn the circles to tell that story and he will then be the only person other than Saint Woody to see the treasure."

"And what do you reckon that treasure is?"

Fergal smiled. If Marshal Blood's information was correct, this tale would now get back to Frank Hunter and hopefully it would entice him out of hiding. He leaned towards Mulhoon and cupped a hand around his ear while lowering his voice to a whisper.

"I don't know for sure, but I have heard it said that the treasure could even be the keys to heaven itself."

Harlan paced back and forth outside of his hotel, fighting down the growing urge to hurry across the road to the law office. An hour had passed since

Fergal and Randolph had left the office and headed to the fort.

As yet there was no sign of Marshal Buckley acting and so he was now sure that the lawman was doing nothing more than just sitting in his office reading reports, again.

Harlan slapped a fist against his thigh as he walked, his frustration growing.

He thought back to the Marshal Blood adventures he'd read. He had to admit those sometimes flagged in the middle, but then Blood always got into a saloon punch-up or fell in love or got attacked by a wild animal, and the story livened up.

But Buckley was doing none of those things.

He could invent yet more danger for him to face to pad out his story, but that wasn't what he wanted to do. He wanted to write about real events.

Unable to contain his irritation any longer he headed across the road to see Buckley. As he had expected, when he arrived the lawman was sitting hunched over the reports that he'd spread across his desk.

"Harlan again," he said without looking up, his tone weary. "The third visit of the day and it's not yet noon."

"I had to come. Your investigation must be proceeding now after you've seen Fergal and Randolph."

"Sure is." Buckley looked up and shrugged. "But I

have nothing to report, as always. I reckon from now on our arrangement should be that I'll be the one who seeks you out when something happens, otherwise you can assume nothing has."

Buckley's monotone drawl suggested this would be an unlikely occurrence.

"But what about . . . ? What about . . . ?" Harlan waved his arms as he searched for the right words. "Something more must have happened, surely."

Buckley sighed. "As I've told you repeatedly, Harlan, Fergal and Randolph are looking for Frank Hunter and their stolen casket of treasure. The gunrunners and the missing Sergeant Woody are a military manner. The only thing I have to investigate is the pig rustling."

"Then investigate!" Harlan snapped, his frustration at Buckley's seeming inactivity finally brimming over.

"I am." Buckley pointed at the statements spread over his desk.

"But reading reports won't solve this case."

"Oh?" Buckley said, raising his eyebrows and folding his arms. "Then I'd be obliged if you could tell me what will."

Harlan gestured to the door. "Now that you're trying to find out where the mystery hog came from, you have to do what I did and go out there and talk to the farmers with missing pigs. Then pick up clues as to where the pigs have gone, look for more escaped hogs, question people eating pork . . . Just do something instead of sitting there reading whatever it is you were reading."

Anger flashed in Buckley's eyes before he got himself under control by looking away and grinding his jaw. He took deep breaths then provided a quick snorting laugh and turned back to him.

"Harlan," he said, leaning forward, "it's taken several days, but now we've finally come full circle. What you are trying to tell me is what I tried to tell you the first time you walked in here, except you didn't believe me then. It boils down to this—real life is a lot duller than it is in the dime novels. Am I right?"

"I guess it is," Harlan murmured, his cheeks warming with embarrassment at his outburst. "But you're the real Marshal Blood. You have adventures. I want to write about one, except there isn't no adventure going on, and I've got no way to end my story."

"You're right. There is adventure aplenty going on in the dime novels." Buckley opened his top drawer and removed a book with a familiar orange cover.

"You're reading a Marshal Blood adventure," Harlan gasped.

"I thought I'd try one, to see what people write about my life." Buckley lowered his tone. "I wasn't impressed."

"Why?"

"Because it's all nonsense." Buckley opened the book and rummaged through it to find a page in the middle. "Take this section for instance. I'm on horseback, chasing after an outlaw who's on foot and running away from me. So what did I do?"

Buckley's question had probably been rhetorical, but Harlan had almost perfect recall of all the Marshal Blood novels. Purely by noting the position Buckley had opened the book, he could work out the passage to which Buckley was referring.

"You drew alongside the outlaw," he said, proud of his knowledge, "leapt off your horse, then grabbed the outlaw around the neck and wrestled him to the ground."

"And did that work?"

"It sure did. The outlaw struggled and nearly got away, but got a punch to the jaw for his trouble."

"Which knocked him cold . . ." Buckley sighed and looked aloft.

"What's wrong with that?"

"For a start, all I would get if I leaped off a galloping horse at a man is a broken leg or two, provided I was lucky enough to actually hit him, because if I missed I'd break my neck." Buckley bunched a fist. "And even if I avoided that mishap the punch I delivered would involve this fragile hand slamming into the outlaw's solid jaw. I would just break my own hand while the outlaw would get away with only a mild bruise, then while the pain of my broken hand made me roll about in agony, he'd escape."

Buckley let his hand go limp, then pushed it back and forth in a mime of having a broken hand.

"Then what should he . . . you have done?"

"Blood should have done what I or any other lawman would do in the that situation. Stay on the horse and round the outlaw up, telling him to stop then lie down on the ground to be searched. If he resisted, I'd shoot him."

"That doesn't sound so interesting."

"It doesn't, but that's real life for you. And then there's this bit." Buckley shuffled the pages on to the next chapter. "I leap off the roof of a speeding train on to my horse, a most obliging steed who somehow worked out it had to gallop alongside the tracks perfectly matching the train's speed. Do I even need to tell you what's wrong with that?"

"It is unlikely, I guess, but what would you have done, bearing in mind the bandits were getting away?"

"Putting aside the fact I'd have never been so reckless as to climb up onto the roof in the first place, I'd have let 'em get away. Then I'd have sat calmly in my seat and waited until the next station where I'd have got off to pursue them with both my legs intact."

"That's a bad idea when you have a lost city of gold to find and only a day to do it in," Harlan murmured, unwilling to accept Buckley was making a valid point.

"So let's consider that deadline." Buckley riffled

through to the end of the book and stabbed a finger on to the last page. "I have just disarmed five bandits with a toothpick and am now free to finally find the lost city of gold. Except my one true love, or at least this book's one true love as I seem to have forgotten about my one true love who was in the previous book, is about to die. The bandit leader has strapped her out on the edge of a precipitous ridge, having conveniently told me where and when he's going to kill her. To save her I have to cross an impassable desert, climb an un-climbable mountain, and—"

"I don't know what you're getting at," Harlan snapped.

Buckley hurled the book on to the desk. "I'm get-ting at the fact you want adventure like it is in the dime novels. You want bandits with poor aim chasing he-roes in stages, and lawmen with great aim shooting guns out of outlaws' hands, but it's not like that. This is real life and in real life lawmen sit around in offices reading reports while they wait for real things to hap-pen. Except sometimes those real things don't happen, and sometimes real life doesn't have endings. Maybe this is one of those occasions."

Harlan shrugged. "If that's the case, how can I ever end my story?"

"In the usual way Marshal Blood adventures end. Stick a pointless gunfight on at the end."

"But that's precisely what I don't want to do."

"Harlan, you don't know what you want to do, but

I know one thing for sure." Buckley leaned forward and lowered his voice, enunciating each word with unaccustomed authority. "You have to accept that what you've seen is all the reality you'll get and you just have to leave me alone now."

Harlan knew Buckley was talking sense. He edged a pace towards the door, then another, but found he couldn't leave his idol without trying one last attempt to talk him round.

"I could do that," he said, lowering his voice to a conciliatory tone, "but I'd still like to keep most of my story real. Randolph and Fergal really do want to reclaim their stolen treasure from Frank Hunter and to locate Saint Woody. They won't rest until they do that, whether I'm writing up their story or not."

For long moments Buckley considered him, then slapped his legs and stood.

"All right, Harlan. You want an ending for your story. I'll give you an ending."

Buckley beckoned for Harlan to follow him then headed outside. He kept up a determined pace as he strode down the road towards the Lazy Sow Saloon.

He stopped outside Fergal's wagon. It was secure and locked, but Buckley paced along looking at its wooden walls until he found a knothole. He looked through the hole, then stepped back and beckoned for Harlan to look.

Harlan put his right eye up to the knothole and looked around inside the wagon, seeing an untidy clutter of crates and boxes piled up.

"What am I looking at?" he asked.

"The large casket in the middle of the wagon."

"I can see it." Harlan looked the casket up and down, noting the rusting metal edges, the jeweled circles on the lid. "It looks just like the casket Fergal described as containing the treasure of Saint Woody."

Buckley sighed then lowered his voice.

"That's because it is it."

Harlan swung round from looking through the hole to face Buckley.

"They've wrested it back from that outlaw Frank Hunter!"

Buckley's eyes narrowed and he opened his mouth to respond then closed it and looked downwards as if he was pondering on whether to provide his original retort.

"It appears they did," he said finally.

"I bet the tale of how they took on that notorious outlaw to reclaim their treasure is a magnificent one."

Buckley raised his head, smiling, and slapped Harlan on the back.

"I'm sure it will be, Harlan. So find Fergal and Randolph, ask them how they did it, then use what they tell you to end your tale."

"I could," Harlan said cautiously. "But what about Saint Woody?"

"I'm sure they've tied up all the loose ends, but in case they haven't," Buckley said raising his voice as he backed away, "just repeat to yourself—'Whatever happens, I will leave Marshal Buckley alone'."

Buckley gave Harlan one last warning glare then turned on his heel and headed back to the law office.

"Whatever happens," Harlan murmured unhappily to himself, "I will leave Marshal Blood alone."

When he'd headed out through the fort gates, Randolph saw Harlan waiting outside their wagon. He conferred with Fergal about what he thought Harlan's pensive pacing up and down meant. They decided that whatever it meant, Fergal should lead.

"What do you want, young Harlan?" Fergal asked when they reached him.

Harlan gestured at the wagon. "To finish my story, with your help."

"I know that, and I'm sure Marshal Buckley can help you there."

"He already has. He's told me the good news."

"Has he?"

"Yeah. You've found the treasure of Saint Woody."

"We have?" Fergal stepped back a pace, frowning, then got himself under control and laid a friendly hand on Harlan's shoulder. "Of course we have. What else did our town marshal tell you?"

"He reckoned you'd also solved the mystery of where Saint Woody is."

"He was being a bit premature, but—"

"That mean you haven't?" Harlan said, frowning.

Fergal considered him, then looked towards the law office, grinding his jaw as he pondered.

"Fergal," Randolph urged, "perhaps we shouldn't keep this news from Harlan. He has a story to write, and I'm sure Marshal Buckley is eager to move on and return to dealing with his normal investigations."

"I'm sure he is." Fergal released his hand and smiled at Harlan. "Yes, Harlan. We have finally solved all the mysteries and tracked down the legendary Saint Woody. In fact, we're about to go and see him now."

"I just knew it. Can I come with you?"

Fergal shot a glance at Randolph, who nodded.

"But of course." Fergal gestured ahead to the wagon, inviting Harlan to join them.

"I'll bring my horse so I can get back," Harlan said, bounding along the boardwalk. "And you must have a great tale to tell of how you reclaimed your treasure from Frank Hunter and worked out where Woody is."

"I must," Fergal murmured. Then, as he warmed to the task at hand, he gripped Harlan's shoulder and halted him. "So bring your manuscript along because our tale is a wondrous one you'll just want to write down quickly."

"I knew it would be," Harlan said before dashing across the road to the hotel.

Fergal and Randolph watched him leave, smiling.

"You know, Fergal, I'm almost as excited as he is to hear this tale."

Chapter Twelve

*F*ergal O'Brien stood in the center of the road with his legs planted wide and his long coat flapping in the light wind that breathed through the deserted ghost town. Thrust over his right shoulder was a spade, his trusty six-shooter at his hip.

Frank Hunter and his three bandit aides had lined up ahead, each man cold-eyed, their hands dangling beside their holsters, while behind them Randolph McDougal lay sprawled against the treasure of Saint Woody, beaten and defeated.

"What have you done with Saint Woody?" Fergal demanded, glaring at Frank before running his gaze over the bandits one at a time.

"You don't ask the questions here, Fergal," Frank muttered.

"Then I'll give you an order. In ten seconds you'll be spitting bullets unless you step away from Randolph."

"The only direction I'm going is out of town in twenty seconds to dig your grave with that there spade."

The bandits laughed, their tones sneering and arrogant.

"You sure got that wrong," Fergal said.

"How?"

Fergal rolled the spade from his shoulder and threw it. The spade turned end over end before slicing blade down into the ground two feet away from Frank's right boot, quivering for a moment before coming to rest.

"Because I don't want you waiting for those twenty seconds before you start digging. I reckon four graves will be enough."

"Am I getting this down right?" Harlan asked.

"You've covered the details excellently so far," Fergal said, peering at Harlan's writing. "Although I believe I had to shoot five men not four when I rescued Randolph."

Harlan made the correction then resumed writing.

As the house Emerson had directed them to was ahead, Harlan was writing Fergal's tale as quickly as he could to get up to date with the developing situation before they finally met Woody.

On the other side of the seat Randolph leaned over to see what Fergal was reading.

"This is very interesting," he said after a moment.

"And," Fergal said, "an accurate retelling of how we reclaimed our treasure from Frank Hunter, isn't it?"

"It sure is," Randolph said in a suitably low and sarcastic tone. "Again I must express my gratitude to you for saving my life by bravely riding into town and shooting up Frank Hunter and all those bandits."

"Anything for my trusted partner."

Randolph drew the horses to a halt twenty yards from the house then released the reins to point at one passage.

"Although I'm not so sure about this part where you swam a raging river, single-handedly wrestled a bear to the ground, then built a raft out of two fallen trees to rescue me from—"

"It wasn't my fault you kept getting into scrapes I had to rescue you from."

"I guess not." Randolph considered the house, noting it was quiet, although a horse and wagon in a corral at the side suggested it was occupied. "And as we have no idea what kind of reception we'll receive here, it might be best if you go up to the house first. You don't want to have to rescue me a third time."

Fergal shot Randolph an irritated glance, but with a rueful smile he acknowledged his tall tale had brought that retaliation on himself and jumped down from the wagon.

Slowly he headed to the house, his paces becoming more uncertain the closer he got to the house as he darted his nervous gaze around.

Randolph watched his worried partner, smiling to himself, then took pity on him. After telling Harlan to stay on the wagon, he jumped down then hurried on to reach the house first.

He raised a hand, but before he could knock on the door, the door opened to reveal a man. He was rangy and dressed in black with an enormous stove hat. Set within his gaunt features were piercing green eyes that appeared to appraise them within seconds.

"Woody?" Fergal asked, looking past Randolph.

"Who wants to know?" the man replied in a drawling but cultured tone.

"Fergal O'Brien and Randolph McDougal. We've traveled across three state lines to find you."

"In that case," the man said, moving to close the door, "I have no idea who this Woody is."

Randolph laughed then planted a firm foot in the door.

"You can't fool us. Sergeant Emerson Dodge sent us."

"We're here to help you," Fergal added.

The man looked at them around the side of the door, while Fergal and Randolph provided their most trustworthy expressions.

"All right," he said finally. "I am Woody."

"Yeehaw," Fergal said while Randolph asked the obvious question.

"Is that Saint Woody, or Sergeant Woody?"

"I am a sergeant now. It has been some years since anyone thought it amusing to call me by that name."

"Why did they?"

"Because," he said, lowering his voice to a funereal tone, "it has been said that I am the furthest a man can get from being a saint."

Silence reigned while they waited for Woody to provide the punch line to what had sounded like a joke, but he maintained a blank expression.

"I guess," Fergal said, breaking the uncomfortable silence, "we've met a few of those before."

"And why do you two want to meet me?"

"Did you make a casket some years ago, perhaps for a traveling show?"

"Perhaps." Woody considered then nodded. "About six feet long, three—"

"That's the one. We have it, except we can't open it."

Woody's eyes opened wide, this being his first change of expression from his somber outlook.

"Why would you want to do that?"

Fergal hesitated, as providing an honest answer would require him to admit he really had hoped there would be treasure inside the casket, but Randolph had no such qualms.

"We had heard the keys to heaven itself are inside."

Woody turned from Fergal to consider him then removed his stove hat and tucked it beneath an arm.

"And in a kind of way that is what is inside. Show me to the casket and I will open it for you."

Fergal and Randolph exchanged a glance that asked each other whether this man was joking. Neither man knew the answer.

So Fergal gestured to his wagon. Then, with he and Randolph walking behind him, Woody set off, walking in a slow and stiff-legged manner with his hat held at his side as if he was escorting a coffin.

"I can't believe we're about to learn the truth," Randolph whispered to Fergal.

"I wouldn't get too hopeful. Look at him. He doesn't exactly look honest."

"The same could be said of us. But even if it's empty, at least we'll know."

Woody stomped his feet as he stopped beside the wagon.

"You ought to hope it is empty," he said.

"What do you mean?" Randolph asked.

While Harlan got down from the wagon and joined them with his mouth open with an awed look, Woody lowered his voice to a graveside pitch and widened his eyes as if he was about to reveal something macabre.

"All will be revealed."

With Harlan's help Randolph hefted the casket

from the wagon. Then, on Woody's instructions, they dragged it into shade beside the house. Randolph stood back to let Woody finally let them see inside.

Woody paced around it in his slow and deliberate manner then put his hat on the ground and flexed his hands before placing them on the jeweled circles.

"Can you do it?" Fergal asked, no longer able to contain his excitement.

"I believe so," Woody said, looking up at him. "You have heard that you have to move these circles to a particular pattern to open it?"

"We have, and that the positions must tell the story of your life."

"That could explain it." He turned the first circle to a new position. "This picture is of a child, for obvious reasons, and the next is of a buzzard."

"Why a buzzard?"

Woody pondered before moving the second circle.

"I guess that represented my . . ."—Woody licked his lips—"my inquisitive nature. The third picture is a man holding a tool, a knife perhaps, a very sharp knife."

"Why a knife?" Randolph asked with an audible gulp.

Woody considered him with his piercing green eyes, making Randolph look away at the casket. He couldn't help but notice that in the first picture, the child's mouth was open, its face contorted as if it were screaming in pain . . .

"Perhaps," Woody said, breaking Randolph away from his uncomfortable thoughts, "the tool is a sword, of the kind a soldier might carry. Then there is the fourth symbol of a hole in the ground, a grave perhaps."

Neither Randolph nor Fergal were interested enough to ask for an explanation of that.

"And finally . . ." Woody said, standing back and gesturing, drawing Randolph's attention to the final circle.

Randolph looked at each of the stylized representations of people and animals, until with a snort to himself he saw the most likely one.

"A pig?" he asked.

"You have got it." With a flourish Woody twirled the final circle to the new position that indicated the pig then slapped his hat back on his head and gestured for Randolph to insert a coin.

As this was likely to be the final time he'd do this, Randolph slipped a dollar into the slot. With hope in his heart he watched the circles turn and listened to the dollar rattle on its circuitous route around the insides of the casket.

When the coin stopped rattling and the circles came to a halt, for the first time Randolph saw they stopped in the same configuration as they had been in before moving. In celebration of this event, a catch within the casket clicked and the lid sprang up a few inches, the motion making the circles spin.

Woody took a long pace backwards while Fergal came over to join Randolph. They both put a hand to the lid and slowly inched it up, more and more of the inside of the casket becoming visible.

To prolong the revelation of the solution to the mystery that had fascinated them for the last six months, Randolph closed his eyes while continuing to lift the lid.

When the lid was perpendicular, Fergal gasped and this encouraged Randolph to open his eyes.

The shining contents inside dazzled him, making him flinch.

He rubbed his eyes, blinking and shocked that the promise of treasure inside the casket had unexpectedly proved to be correct. He glanced at Woody and saw that he was smiling, although he'd only bared his teeth—his eyes remained blank.

Beside him, Fergal was chuckling to himself.

"Look again," Fergal said.

Randolph looked back inside the casket, noting the dazzling blueness, the shifting patches of white . . .

He winced then looked up at the blue sky above, marred only by a few clouds. Then he peered down into the casket, his perspective changing to let him see that nothing was inside the casket aside from the highly polished sides and base.

"It's empty, after all," he said, disappointed now.

Looking more carefully he saw that the visible sides were set in from the actual sides to give room for the mechanism that rolled the coins around in an intriguing manner.

But aside from that there was nothing inside the casket.

"What were you expecting?" Woody asked. "The keys to heaven itself?"

"It had been rumored."

"But that is only because it is true." Woody gave a low laugh, the sound again containing no emotion. "Look more carefully."

Randolph peered down into the casket again, but saw only the reflection of the sky in the base. He was about to ask Woody what he had meant, but then he noticed the only flaw in the shiny surfaces.

He peered closer and saw that there was tiny writing on the base of the casket. Intrigued now he lowered his head to read it, placing a hand on the lip to steady himself, but the lip was so smooth his hand slipped and he tumbled forward, half-falling into the casket.

He waved his arms to extricate himself, but his sudden movement dislodged the lid and it banged against the back of his head, knocking him downwards a second time. By the time he'd extricated himself the lid had closed, almost trapping his fingers, and everyone but Woody was laughing at his ungainly predicament.

"What did it say?" Fergal asked between chuckles.

"I didn't see," Randolph said, rubbing his head, "and I'm not wasting my time trying to read it again."

Fergal looked at Woody, who shrugged.

"It is a message for anyone who ever manages to open the casket," he said.

"Which is?" Fergal asked.

Woody ran his fingers along the top of the casket, swirling the circles round.

"Banging on the lid will not work."

"What kind of message is that?"

Woody finished turning the circles, leaving them in the position that would let it open.

"A very useful one to reduce distress when people go looking for those keys to heaven." Woody looked at each person in turn, but when everyone continued to look at him in a bemused manner he coughed. "Then just put it down to my own particular brand of humor."

He firmed his expression from its usual somber state to one of statue-like forbearance as if humor was the last thing that'd ever enter his thoughts.

"Very unusual," Fergal said. "But certainly not worth us lugging it around for six months trying to find you."

"That is not my problem. So now that I have helped you, how will you help me?"

Randolph noted Woody had lowered his tone to its lowest yet, implying that whatever they had to say it wouldn't interest him, but if he noticed, Fergal didn't show it as he placed a hand on Woody's shoulder.

Woody glanced at the hand touching him, his lip curling with distaste, but Fergal didn't remove it.

"I have a proposition," he said, "a very profitable proposition."

Chapter Thirteen

*N*ot only were his friends in danger but now the legendary Saint Woody was too.

That thought reverberated the loudest through Marshal Blood's mind as he peered out through the window of the abandoned saloon.

Frank Hunter's bandit gang was out there, as was the trigger-happy Major Mulhoon. Between them they had placed guns behind every window and on every false-fronted roof of this abandoned ghost town.

He would need to take on at least a dozen men and his chances of making it back to Fort Arlen alive were almost nonexistent, but that didn't waver him from his intent.

"Nobody threatens my friends and lives," he muttered to himself.

Then, with calm determination Marshal Blood strapped on his six-shooter, drew down the brim of his hat, and headed out onto the windswept road.

Harlan was right.

This was a terrible thing for Marshal Ed Buckley to admit to himself as he rode towards Christopher Tate's farm, but his young follower had correctly deduced his attitude.

He did spend too much time in the law office rather than trying to make the best job he could out of the few cases he did have. Even when a real piece of trouble had come along in the form of the gun-runners, a few harsh words from Major Mulhoon had cowed him into submission.

But no more.

He had resolved to find out where that hog in the fort had come from using systematic, dogged investigation. Already he'd visited ten farms and confirmed that their hogs were either all accounted for or if any had been rustled they didn't match the description of the rogue hog.

His meandering farm visits had encouraged Major Mulhoon and a group of troopers to tail him, but they were keeping their distance.

This time Buckley would have welcomed meeting

him. An idea was forming in his mind as to what had been happening in Fort Arlen, and it was one he'd enjoy explaining to the gun-toting major.

"Marshal Buckley," Christopher said, waving to him when he pulled up outside his dugout. "I haven't seen you out here in a while."

"I know, but I've been busy investigating the disappearance of all those pigs."

"A sorry business indeed," Christopher murmured, sniffing with suppressed emotion as Buckley dismounted.

"So I'd be obliged if you could answer a question." Buckley withdrew the wanted poster from his pocket. "Have you seen this pig?"

Christopher looked at the poster, shaking his head, but then his eyes opened wider and he took the paper from Buckley. He held it up to the light then stabbed a finger against the distinctive blotch beneath the hog's right eye.

"It looks a bit like . . . but no. That one disappeared a year ago."

"A year? But that was long before the rustling started." Buckley rubbed his chin as he pondered, this revelation adding an extra dimension to his theory, and as if in support of that belief, he noted that Mulhoon was now approaching the farm. "Or maybe he was the first."

"If it is him, he's grown a lot. I'll show you what I mean. I'll fetch his youngest."

While Christopher went inside, Major Mulhoon drew up. Buckley swung round to face him, this time determined not to let himself be cowed.

"Are you following me?"

Mulhoon, with his six troopers behind him, sat tall in the saddle.

"When there's gun-runners on the loose I follow anybody who's moving about, and you've done more moving than most today."

"I have, and it's been worth the effort. I'm getting close to uncovering the truth about what's been happening here."

"Which is?"

Buckley pointed at Christopher, who was emerging from his house with a piglet under one arm. He couldn't help but notice the blotch on its face.

"This is the evidence," Buckley said, "that proves you've got a whole heap of things wrong around here."

"A pig?"

Buckley gestured at Christopher, asking him to give him the piglet, and with some reluctance Christopher handed it over.

"Not just any pig." Buckley held the squirming animal aloft. Its little legs whirled while it proved its lungs were in better order than its bladder. "This one has a distinctive blotch on its face that it inherited from its father, a father who went missing a year ago before he turned up in your fort last week."

"What has that got to do with the gun-runners?"

Although he now believed there were no gun-runners, Buckley wasn't sure of all the details yet. So he waved his arms vaguely as he searched for the right words and his motion made the piglet screech then squirm out of his hands.

The little piglet hit the ground with its legs paddling and set off, running away from the house and straight for Mulhoon's horse, which backed away in fright.

Christopher shouted out for the piglet to come back but it ignored him and ran between the horse's legs, its squawking making the horse rear.

Without even thinking, Mulhoon drew his gun and turned in the saddle to blast lead down into the animal as it emerged. The piglet squeaked once then rolled over to lie on its side.

An agonizingly painful screech tore from Christopher's lips. Then he hurried off, skidding to a halt on his side beside the animal. He lay a hand on its still flank, but it didn't react, then glared up at Mulhoon.

"You varmint," he muttered, getting to his feet and cuddling the dead animal to his chest with one hand.

Tenderly he set the piglet down then paced up to Mulhoon's horse and lunged for the major's leg.

Mulhoon flailed his leg, trying to keep it away from Christopher's grasp, but Christopher grabbed a good hold of his knee and tugged, dragging Mulhoon from his saddle for him to land in an ungainly heap on the ground.

Before Mulhoon could get his wits about him Christopher pulled him to his feet and put all his pent-up anger behind a solid blow to Mulhoon's jaw that sent him reeling. Then he turned on his heel and stormed back to his house, wringing his hand.

Buckley could see the tears running down Christopher's face and he moved to intercept him and offer his condolences, but Christopher broke into a run, moving to slip by him. Christopher's hand jerked towards his pocket, reaching for a kerchief to dry his tears.

A gunshot tore out. Christopher fell to his knees.

Buckley swung round to see that Mulhoon was on one knee, smoke rising from his gun, having shot the unarmed farmer in the back. He turned back towards Christopher to see him stagger to his feet and manage a stumbling pace towards his house.

Buckley tried to move towards the wounded man to help him, but found that the shock had rooted him to the spot.

Then a second shot tore into Christopher's back and sent him spinning into the house.

"No more!" Buckley shouted, finally forcing himself to move between Christopher and the gun-toting major.

Then, while waving his arms, he backed away into the dugout to find Christopher lying on his side. So much blood marred his back he didn't think anyone could help him.

With dozens of bustling pigs looking on, their small

eyes conveying their concern and their fright, he turned him over and held him up against a raised knee. Christopher looked up, his eyes already clouding.

"Look after my little ones for me," he whispered, then flopped.

Buckley lowered him to the ground, shocked at the sudden disastrous turn of events that had transformed a peaceful situation into carnage in a matter of moments.

He stood and with the squealing of the pigs echoing behind him he paced out from the dugout to face the advancing Mulhoon. An odd mixture of anger and fear churned in his stomach.

"Is he dead?" Mulhoon demanded.

"Yeah," Buckley said. "But you didn't need to shoot him. Christopher wasn't a gun-runner."

Mulhoon shrugged. "His hand was going to his pocket, perhaps for a hidden gun."

"He wasn't going for his gun. He was going for his kerchief!"

"I wasn't to know that."

Buckley sighed. "Just leave."

"Not before you tell me what you've found out."

Buckley took deep breaths to calm himself then waved a dismissive hand at Mulhoon.

"Ask Sergeant Emerson Dodge."

Harlan laid down his pen, feeling an odd mixture of disappointment and delight after finally writing up the details he'd obtained today.

After returning to his hotel room, he'd had no choice but to use a mixture of second-hand testimony and poetic licence to liven up events that weren't as interesting as he'd hoped they would be.

It was now late in the day and the weekly train was due in before sundown. He still didn't have an ending for his story, but as he'd seen everything he could see to help him, and he'd spent all of his money, he packed up his manuscript. Then he booked out of the hotel and trudged off.

Out on the boardwalk he cast a last lingering look at the law office, which appeared to be unoccupied.

"Whatever happens," he said to himself, remembering Buckley's last words to him, "I will leave Marshal Buckley alone."

Then he set off down the road.

When he arrived at the station he discovered that the train back east was due in another hour, but he decided to wait here.

After all, there was nothing left for him in Fort Arlen.

So he sat on a bench and looked around idly, biding his time.

Presently a cortege of officers rode into town led by Major Mulhoon. At the back one man was lying face down over a horse.

"The gun-runners must have struck," Harlan said to himself, intrigue making his heart beat faster.

He looked down the tracks and told himself that he

did need to leave town now. But as the train's arrival was still thirty minutes away, he stood and headed over to the fort, hoping to get one last authentic detail for his story.

By the time he arrived the troopers had gone into the fort.

He couldn't see who had been killed, but in a surprisingly poor show of discipline they'd left the gates open, letting him see Major Mulhoon dismount and confront Sergeant Dodge.

A fierce argument ensued with much gesticulating, in which Mulhoon's angry arm-jerks and finger-pointing conveyed he would shoot someone if he didn't get his way.

Worryingly, Harlan got the impression from the significant gesturing at the dead man that he was someone who had defied Mulhoon. The tirade went on for some time until finally Emerson nodded then muttered a one-word answer and pointed westwards.

This appeased Mulhoon and he mounted up. With Emerson at his side and his West Point officers behind him, he headed out through the gates.

"Onwards, men," Mulhoon called out as he passed Harlan. "It's time to bring Woody to justice."

Harlan backed away from the gates, trying to piece together what he'd learned. His conclusion was a worrying one.

Emerson had told Mulhoon where Woody was, so Mulhoon was going after him. Even though Woody was clearly not involved in the gun-running, with the tension haven risen after the death, that didn't bode well for his quarry, and perhaps for Fergal and Randolph too.

"Whatever happens," Harlan said, "I will leave Marshal Buckley alone."

This time that didn't feel right.

So as soon as Mulhoon and the troopers had galloped off, Harlan ran back into town. Buckley's horse was now standing outside the law office so he headed there first, but when he pushed open the door he faced a deserted room.

He was about to close the door and go in search of him when he heard murmuring. He edged inside and looked around, not seeing any sign of anyone until he noticed the open door to the small jailhouse at the back.

One cautious pace at a time, he walked to the door and peered inside. Buckley was sitting on a cot in a cell, his arms wrapped around the legs he'd drawn up to his chin, rocking back and forth and murmuring to himself.

"I know you told me to leave you alone," Harlan said, "but this crisis is getting really serious now. Major Mulhoon is all set to go and arrest Woody."

Buckley looked up and provided a sneering smile, although he didn't stop rocking.

"Best news I've heard all day."

Harlan shook himself, presuming he'd misheard.

"You don't understand. With Mulhoon leading there's sure to be plenty of shooting and Randolph and Fergal are with Woody."

"But I do understand." Buckley released his legs to slap the cot. "That's why I'm staying here."

"Fergal and Randolph are your friends and—"

"You have no idea how dangerous Major Mulhoon is. He shot up a farmer when his piglet got loose. Nobody stands up to him, and certainly not a man like me who couldn't even bring a pig rustler to justice."

Harlan opened and closed his mouth soundlessly, struggling to find the words to express himself.

"But you're Marshal Blood!" he shouted, finally finding his voice.

"I am not Marshal Blood!"

"I don't understand."

Buckley held his head in his hands. "What is there to understand? I had a chance today to finally become the lawman I wanted to be. I sifted through the evidence, put it together, and worked out what was happening and who was guilty. But then when Major Mulhoon started shooting I was too slow to react and now Christopher is dead."

"I'm sure that wasn't your fault."

"It wasn't, but that doesn't make it any easier." Buckley sniffed then rubbed at his nose. "If I were a lawman like Marshal Blood, somehow I'd have found the right thing to do."

Harlan sighed. "So it's turned full circle again and

I'm now the one who has to tell you that real life is different to the dime novels."

"I know that. But look at me." Buckley pointed at himself with a shaking hand. "I'm no lawman. I'm too scared to go and arrest the guilty people just because of Major Mulhoon."

Although Buckley's reticence to do his duty bemused Harlan, he sat on the cot facing him and smiled sympathetically.

"I guess it must be hard to be the man who always has to face up to the gun-toting outlaws. But someone has to do it to stop evil triumphing."

Buckley took a deep breath. "You trying to tell me that no matter how scared I am, I'm a lawman with a duty to perform and I have to go and face up to Major Mulhoon?"

"You do."

"And not just to get you an ending for your story?"

"I don't have one but that doesn't matter. I saw the dead man. I know this is for real."

"As real as it gets," Buckley murmured, looking at his shaking hand. He gripped it tightly to stop the shaking. Then he got to his feet, drew his gunbelt higher, and made his slow way to the cell door. He stopped in the doorway and looked back at Harlan. "I'm leaving now. Duty calls."

"Can I come?"

"You might as well, and bring plenty of paper to write this up." Buckley set off through the door. "Marshal Blood's last adventure should be faithfully recorded."

"You can offer me propositions all day and all night," Woody said, shaking his head. "But you will never find one that will tempt me."

Fergal's legendary ability to negotiate deals had hit a wall with the taciturn Woody. Worse, Woody had claimed the casket for himself and to show how determined he was, he'd dragged it into the house and sat on it.

"Except," Fergal said, "I can offer you something very special indeed—life."

"Life can be marginally more interesting than death."

Despite his odd comment Fergal gave Randolph a significant look. If he had to admit defeat, the look said, they would still leave with the casket, whether by negotiation or by the more likely method of Fergal distracting Woody while Randolph made off with it.

While Fergal pondered on his next line of attack, Randolph looked around the bare room, noting that aside from the main door, there was one other door to an internal room. Draped on a hook beside the door was a uniform, at least confirming Woody intended to return to his military duties one day.

"Death may come sooner than you think," Fergal said, matching Woody's usual grave tone, "when your adversary is a military man like Major Rory

Shoot-em-up Mulhoon, a man who shoots while he's distracting you with a question."

"I have everything I need to defend myself in here," Woody said.

Woody stared at Fergal. When his frank gaze made Fergal uncomfortable, he joined Randolph in looking around the room. His gaze also stopped to consider the only internal door.

He paced over to the door then threw it open with a flourish. He didn't look inside but gestured into the other room and raised his eyebrows.

"And these will save you, will they?"

From inside the room squealing and rustling sounded, letting Randolph deduce Woody was keeping the stolen pigs in there.

"I do not mean the meat. I mean the casket." Woody tapped the lid. "Now I have it back, I need nothing else to defend myself."

"It's not big enough to hide behind," Fergal said, smiling. "Believe me, we've tried."

"You should not have tried hiding behind it but . . . outside." Woody stood and placed a hand beside his ear.

"I don't know what you . . ." Fergal narrowed his eyes when he saw that Woody was shaking his head with a hand cupped beside his ear. "What's wrong?"

"I mean I am listening, but not to you. I believe we will soon enjoy the company of the visitor of which you have spoken."

Randolph strained his hearing, but heard nothing other than the pigs squealing next door.

"Who?" Fergal asked.

Woody nodded towards the door and so Randolph hurried to the window to look out. Sure enough, riders were approaching, although they were still a quarter-mile away. He watched them closely until he confirmed they were Major Mulhoon and his team of West Point officers.

"Major Mulhoon I presume," Woody said, although from where he was standing he couldn't see through the window.

"In that case, now is the right time for that deal," Fergal said. "We'll get you out of here alive for fifty percent of everything you'll ever get from this setup."

Randolph sighed. "If you don't take Fergal's offer, based on Major Mulhoon's reputation, that'll be about twenty bullets apiece."

"I have a better offer," Woody said. "I will get you out of here alive for fifty percent of everything you will ever get from the treasure of Saint Woody."

Fergal and Randolph both stared at Woody, noting he wasn't armed, noting the bare room, while listening to the pigs squeal next door.

To avoid looking too confused, Randolph peered through the window to see that outside Major Mulhoon and his team had dismounted. They were now drawing their guns while spreading out before the house.

Sergeant Dodge was amongst them and he was the

only one not to have drawn a gun, but his bowed head and hangdog expression suggested they'd get no help from him.

"You in the house," Mulhoon shouted, standing in full view beside a fence, twenty yards from the door. "What are you doing?"

"It's getting serious," Randolph said. "He's asking questions."

"You have to accept our offer now," Fergal said, glancing at Woody, who still stood beside the casket, as unconcerned and disinterested in the rapidly developing situation as he had been since they'd met him.

"But my own fifty percent offer still stands," Woody said, then gave a small yawn.

"I'm almost tempted to say yes," Fergal said, "just to see how you'll take on a dozen trigger-happy troopers who are armed to the teeth and ready to drill holes in anything that moves."

"Then say it," Randolph said, drawing his gun, "because I don't like these odds."

Fergal stared at the impassive Woody for a moment longer then shook his head and hurried over to join Randolph.

"He's bluffing. So we have to think of something."

Fergal looked at Randolph who, to avoid replying that he had no ideas, risked looking out. He saw that Mulhoon and his men were all in position to mount their assault with guns drawn and trained on the house, then darted back.

"And to think this day started so well when you found out that you'd cured a pig." Randolph uttered a rueful laugh.

"I did, didn't I?" Fergal said, brightening as he looked at the door to the other room, from where a steady mixture of squeals and grunts was emerging. "Although if I remember it right, that cured pig wasn't quite so happy when it first tasted my tonic."

Chapter Fourteen

*B*ullets flew in all directions, closely followed by the bodies.

In the center of the death-dealing maelstrom was the whirling dervish of righteous anger that was Marshal Colt T Blood.

The lawman's trigger finger burned from the hot lead he blasted into the outlaws. Each shot bit with the speed of an enraged rattler and was twice as deadly.

When the gunsmoke cleared, bodies lay draped over barrels, folded over window sills, or in Frank Hunter's case lay sprawled in the center of the road. Only one man remained standing to face him: Major Rory Mulhoon, the deadliest and sneakiest critter of them all.

"Major Mulhoon," Marshal Blood muttered, "I've just wiped out that ugly pig Frank Hunter. Now it's time for you to say your prayers. Those keys to heaven are a-calling."

"I don't pray," Mulhoon said, settling his stance.

"Then that just confirms," Blood said, matching Mulhoon's posture, "that you'll be going to the other place."

Marshal Ed Buckley slowed as he closed on Woody's house, seeing Major Mulhoon and his men lined up ahead.

His palms were sweaty and his heart beat an insistent rhythm at the thought of facing up to the gun-toting major so soon after Christopher Tate's tragic death, but Harlan had been right.

This was the only way he could put that failure behind him.

He had now admitted to himself that back at the farm he had been at best weak and at worst something of a yellow belly. Either way, Christopher had paid the price for his failure to react decisively, but no others would suffer, he had resolved.

He gave Harlan a quick order to stay back and out of trouble, then jumped down from his horse.

"Major Mulhoon," he shouted, "get away from the house and leave this to me."

Mulhoon turned his steely gaze on him and sneered.

"A lawman who spends his life chasing after pig rustlers can't order me to do anything."

Buckley set his feet wide apart and placed his hands on his hips.

"Then maybe he should, because pig rustlers is all you're chasing after."

"What do you mean?"

Buckley snorted. "I mean you've spent all your time since you arrived in Fort Arlen searching for gun-runners, except there are no gun-runners." Buckley looked past Mulhoon at Emerson Dodge. "Sergeant Woody is in there, but the only crime he's committed involves pigs."

While Emerson winced, Mulhoon shook his head.

"And you figured that out all on your own, did you?"

"Sure did, so step aside and let me get the stolen pigs out of there. There'll be no more pig rustling in my town while I'm marshal."

Mulhoon looked over his shoulder at his officers, encouraging them to share in his derision.

"I'm tempted to let you go in there and get all shot up by the gun-runners."

"And I'm tempted to let you go in there and get yourself a good pork dinner."

Mulhoon stayed staring at Buckley for a moment longer then shook his head and turned away.

"I've wasted enough time on you when there's gun-runners to be found." Mulhoon stood before the house with his gun drawn and trained on the door. "You men in there. Come out now and die."

Buckley glanced back at Harlan to make sure he was staying out of danger, then paced towards Mulhoon, determined not to let him deal with this matter in his usual trigger-happy manner.

Then the door swung open, although nobody emerged.

With a triumphant grunt, Mulhoon silently gestured to his men to move in and take up flanking positions on either side of the door. When they were in position he held up three fingers then lowered those fingers one at a time, but he stopped with one finger still held up.

The men by the door shot him a glance, questioning why he was delaying his order to begin firing, then flinched when they saw the reason.

Someone was coming out of the door and he was huge, pink, and annoyed.

The hog stopped beyond the doorway, darting its small wild eyes around while it pawed the ground, foam dripping from its mouth, its angry stance strangely similar to the stance of the wild hog in the fort last week.

Nobody moved as the hog took another slow pace forward, but then a loud grunt sounded from within the house and two more hogs, both even larger and angrier than the first hog came bundling out. They barged into the leading hog, which lurched forward, grunting wildly.

Then they all charged.

The leading hog ran straight on, heading for Mulhoon while the next two splayed out, pounding on towards the flanking men.

The brave West Point officers had been trained to stand their ground no matter how heavily armed the foe and no matter how outnumbered they were, but a half-ton heap of marauding pork was a different matter. The men dived to the side, rolled then came up running.

Several officers, who were lucky enough not to be standing before the pounding hogs, snorted with derision, then silenced when the next wave of pink retribution thundered out of the house.

As self-preservation triumphed over bravery, Randolph emerged and began firing into the air to add to the confusion.

Mulhoon stood his ground, showing no qualms about shooting down an unarmed hog, but unlike a man, the hog running towards him didn't have enough sense to let the bullets ripping into it deter its progress.

It ploughed onwards then at the last moment lowered its head and jerked upwards, sending its snout and short-tusks upwards at Mulhoon's legs. Mulhoon folded over the pig's head, rolled over its body and landed in an undignified sprawling heap on the ground.

Luckily the pig didn't hold a grudge and ran onwards, looking for its next victim.

Unfortunately the nearest person beyond Mulhoon

was Buckley, who backed away while glancing at Mulhoon, seeing him get up, even though he was favoring his right leg, then run for his life.

Buckley decided that for once the major had the right idea. He turned then ran on towards Harlan, hearing hooves pound as the hog closed.

"Move," he said, grabbing his arm. "Nobody stays around when there's a stampede."

"I've read about stampedes in the Marshal Blood adventures," Harlan said, eyeing the advancing hog, "but not one with pigs . . ."

"Quit telling me what you've read about." Buckley pointed out the West Point officers, who were now all scurrying away, the mixture of Randolph's high gunfire and the rampaging wave of pink vengeance making them abandon their duty. "This is as real as it gets. Run for your life!"

Harlan turned to join Buckley in his flight, but when he set off his foot caught in a root and he tripped, making him go to one knee, then fell forward to land on his chest.

Buckley skidded to a halt and turned to see Harlan lying in the path of the charging hog, then did the only thing he could do. He ran back to him, drawing his gun.

The hog loomed just feet away from trampling Harlan into the dirt. A gunshot failed to halt it, and so with no other way to save him Buckley threw himself into the hog's path.

He felt as if he'd run into a solid wall, and worse a solid wall that was running towards him, but he still managed to thrust a stiffened leg to the ground to act as a pivot then shoved. He veered the hog's motion to the side and away from the sprawling Harlan before its frantic pounding hooves tumbled him backwards.

Buckley landed on his back taking the hog with him and heard a sickening crack sound in his chest. Then the hog trampled him, not caring where its hooves landed, blasting all the air from his lungs.

For several seconds his vision darkened but then the weight pressing down on his gun hand loosed out a shot from his gun, blasting a hot surge of lead up into the animal from point-blank range.

With a last crunch of a hoof against his right leg, the weight rolled away, leaving him lying on his back looking up at the sky.

Lightness and darkness flittered before Buckley's eyes while a general numbness overcame him until Harlan's face swam into view, peering down at him.

"Are you all right?" he asked, shock contorting his face.

Buckley felt as if he'd been trampled so heavily he ought to be lying underground.

"I am now I can see you're fine." Buckley experimented with moving and found that his limbs worked.

"That hog almost ran me down, but you pushed it

out of the way then took the full force yourself. You saved my life."

"That's my job, Harlan," he said, finding that after the earlier disaster back at Christopher's dugout those words sounded good.

Buckley tentatively raised himself up on an elbow, but when he'd levered himself to a sitting position and was resting against the back of the dead pig, a sharp pain announced itself in his chest. He probed his torso, wincing.

"Are you injured?" Harlan asked.

Buckley pointed at his chest and put on his best Marshal Blood-type accent.

"Got a bust rib, but I'll be fine."

He looked around. The hogs had done a good job of dispersing the West Point officers. He counted seven running away, and several were lying on the ground in a similar trampled state to the one he was in, including Sergeant Dodge.

Fergal emerged from the house to join Randolph in checking on the injured. He produced a bottle of amber liquid from a small black bag, although Randolph's shaking of the head suggested he didn't think the universal remedy to cure all ills would be successful on hog-trampled men.

Of Major Rory Mulhoon, there was no sign.

"Time to give yourselves up, Sergeant Woody," Major Mulhoon said, stepping into the house.

Woody raised his hands without comment, although he did so in a casual manner as if he'd just decided to give his arms an airing.

"Why should I?" Woody said.

"Why should I . . . ?"

Woody sneered. "I have heard about your interest in military protocol but I believe authority and respect are different matters. Although you have the former, you do not command the latter."

"Then I'll add insubordination to your charges."

"And what charges can you possibly level at me?"

Mulhoon snorted. "I presume that comment means you're planning to tell me what Marshal Buckley tried to say, that you were just stealing meat, and not rifles."

"Is that a question?"

Mulhoon chuckled. "I have a reputation, I know, but I will get to the truth about your gun-running, somehow."

"I have heard that you always find the trouble you are searching for, so I will save you the effort and admit it. I was gun-running."

"I knew it." Mulhoon clenched a fist in triumph, then opened the hand and pointed at Woody. "Give me all the names and details and you'll live for long enough to face a court-martial."

"But I don't need to. You had worked it all out the first time you heard about me." Woody stepped back a pace to let Morton see the casket by the wall. "I stole the rifles on my own and transported them in here."

Mulhoon signified with a raised hand that Woody should not move again, then paced over to the treasure of Saint Woody.

He raised the lid, then narrowed his eyes. The light was poor and he couldn't see anything inside, but slowly his eyes became accustomed to the gloom and although he couldn't see any rifles, there was something inside.

He leaned closer, seeing beams and . . . He looked up at the beams in the ceiling then glared down into what he now saw to be the highly polished metal insides reflecting the ceiling.

"A trick," he murmured, but he wasn't disappointed as he swirled round to confront Woody. "I'll make you regret that many times over."

"No trick," Woody said, his low tone silky and enticing. "Look again."

Mulhoon was about to slam the lid down, but then from the corner of his eye he saw there was something on the bottom of the casket, after all. He lowered his head, one hand holding on to the lid, the other gripping the rim, and peered down into the casket.

He saw writing but it was too small to read and so he lowered his head.

"Banging on the lid will not—" Rapid footfalls sounded a moment before a solid blow hit him behind his right ear and he tumbled forward.

Chapter Fifteen

*W*hen Saint Woody stepped back, the light blasting out from inside the casket dazzled them all.

"I have never seen so much treasure," Fergal O'Brien murmured.

"So the legend was real," Randolph McDougal said, "after all."

Marshal Blood turned from the casket to cast his gaze over the bodies that were sprawled in the road, each outlaw having fallen where either Marshal Blood or his trusted friends had shot them.

He noted that Frank Hunter and his worthless associates had suffered the same fate as

176

always befell his type: Being abandoned to feed the buzzards in a forgotten ghost town.

"It was," he said, "but was the treasure worth all these deaths?"

Neither Fergal nor Randolph could answer, both men being humbled by the carnage they'd had to mete out, leaving the lawman to look down into the casket alone, taking in the shining contents.

With the fortune inside still not cheering him, he looked up to speak with Saint Woody. He blinked to regain his sight after the treasure had dazzled him, but when the after-images had faded away, he couldn't see this most wondrous of individuals.

"He's gone," Randolph said, joining him in looking around and confirming that Woody had disappeared as mysteriously as he had arrived.

"And he's left us with his treasure," Fergal said.

"What can we ever do with it all?"

"My dear friend," Fergal said, placing a hand on Randolph's shoulder, "we must give it to the poor, the destitute, the deserving."

As Randolph murmured his approval of this plan, Marshal Blood sighed with relief, pleased now that two honest and worthy men had become the final owners of the treasure of Saint Woody.

"Will it stop the pain?" Sergeant Dodge asked.

"Of course," Fergal said, holding out the bottle of tonic. "Take one sip of my universal remedy to cure all ills and you'll forget all about your pain."

"I'll try it, then." The grateful trooper reached out with a shaking hand but Fergal withdrew the bottle.

"And all for . . ." Fergal looked around, weighing up the level of suffering around him, "for five dollars a bottle."

"I thought you charged a dollar."

Fergal turned to go. "If you're not interested, there are others in need."

"Just give it to me," Emerson snapped, making Fergal turn back. He took the tonic, after which Fergal moved on to the next trampled man.

Randolph watched the unfortunate Emerson take his first sip, noting he was about to forget about the pain of being trampled. But before the tonic introduced Emerson to a new set of pains, this time in the stomach, Woody emerged from the house, walking at his usual funereal pace.

"Is Mulhoon still in there?" Randolph asked him.

"I have no idea," Woody said, shrugging. "Perhaps he is too embarrassed to come out now he knows he was chasing after phantom gun-runners."

Randolph looked at the house. He hadn't heard

anyone leave and it wasn't like Major Mulhoon to be reticent. Then he searched the horizon for any sign of him, but aside from a few sheepish troopers dawdling back to the house while still looking out for rampaging hogs, he saw nobody.

With Fergal not needing his help to harass the afflicted and Woody offering no more comments, he walked slowly to the house then glanced inside.

Aside from the treasure of Saint Woody standing beside the wall, the room was empty.

He slipped inside, keeping his back to the wall, and headed to the other room to consider the mostly empty pigpens. Then he turned to look around the main room.

Standing quietly he heard an insistent noise that sounded like weak tapping or perhaps scratching. But he couldn't tell if the noise was either being made by the pigs rooting about nearby, or if it was the distant footfalls of someone running away.

Presently the sound stopped. So he shrugged and left the room to join Fergal in ministering to the injured, who had become so desperate for treatment that the tonic was now fetching ten dollars a bottle.

An hour after the siege and pig stampede at Woody's house, Randolph and Fergal arrived back at Fort Arlen.

As soon as they'd drawn the wagon up outside the saloon, Randolph hurried round to the back of the wagon. He directed Harlan, who had been sitting with the injured lawman on the journey back, to go and find a doctor.

"You'll be fine," Randolph said when Harlan had hurried off and he had joined Buckley in the back of the wagon.

"I will be." Buckley reached up to grab Randolph's collar and drew himself up. "Make sure your partner doesn't feed me his tonic so I can stay that way. Those troopers looked in a bad way."

"I promise."

"But then again I shouldn't complain. I never expected to live when I faced up to Major Mulhoon. In fact, where is that gun-toting fool?"

Buckley craned his neck to look out of the back of the wagon, but Randolph pried his fingers from his collar then bade him to lie back down. Then he looked out the wagon at the bedraggled line of troopers heading into the fort.

Most of the West Point officers had made their way back, but although they still looked too embarrassed to head this way and talk about the incident, Randolph guessed that Major Mulhoon's career had taken a severe knock.

"I don't know," he said. "He doesn't appear to have returned to face whatever punishment he's due."

"And he's not the only one facing plenty of that. When Dodge stops groaning about his bellyache, he and Sergeant Woody will have to answer some serious charges."

"In the end you solved the crime you set out to solve." Randolph looked at Buckley, asking the obvious question with his raised eyebrows.

Buckley sighed. "I have, but you two won't be facing no charges from me. I now know you weren't pig rustling. You were probably involved in a whole heap of other stuff, but not pig rustling."

"And that other stuff doesn't concern you?"

"It would only concern a lawman."

Randolph was about to ask what this cryptic comment meant, but Harlan then returned with the doctor.

With Harlan's help, the doctor maneuvered Buckley on to a makeshift stretcher. They took him into the comfort of his law office where they placed him on a cot in the cell in which he and Fergal had resided last week.

While the doctor fussed around him, Randolph took the opportunity to ask his interrupted question.

"A lawman?"

"I'm resigning," Buckley said.

"To do what?" Harlan asked, darting forward to stand over Buckley.

Buckley swung his gaze round to him.

"Thanks to you, Harlan, I've now found my calling, and it's not being a lawman. Now, no more questions and leave me with the doctor."

Harlan backed away to let the doctor do his work, although he refused to leave Buckley until he knew he'd be all right.

Randolph left them. When he arrived back at the wagon he found Fergal and Sergeant Woody in conference.

"I am leaving town too," Woody was saying when Randolph joined them, "before that lawman gets well enough to arrest me."

"So if you're giving up being a soldier, what will you do?" Fergal asked.

"You already know the answer to that because you were right. The future is with showmen such as yourself."

"And what will you show?" Fergal asked, his low tone suggesting he'd already worked out the answer.

Woody roved his gaze to the back of his own wagon and the casket he'd strapped there. They'd had to accept his help in transporting it to town so they'd have the room to bring Buckley.

"The treasure of Saint Woody, of course."

"You can't show that. It's ours."

"I believe the man who made it has more of a right to show it than you two, but let us not quibble. I agreed to take fifty percent of everything we could make from the casket if I got you out of that tricky situation alive, and I did."

"I believe my plan to enrage the pigs with my tonic saved us."

"As I said, let us not quibble about who saved who from whom. The more important fact to discuss is my offer for you to share the profits from the casket."

Fergal shrugged. "If we're doing that, I have to say that fifty percent of what we make isn't worth discussing."

"That is only because you have been using it in the wrong way." Woody widened his eyes. "I know the right way to use it."

"Which is?"

"You have been persuading people to put a dollar in the casket in the hope of winning the keys to heaven itself, but you can get them to give you all their money just to avoid winning those keys."

"I don't understand."

Woody bared his teeth with a wide smile that didn't reach his eyes, then lowered his tone.

"Come with me, gentlemen, and I will show you how."

Without further comment Woody raised the reins and trundled his wagon towards the edge of town.

Randolph jumped up on to the seat beside Fergal to watch him leave.

"Are we chasing after him to get back our property? Or are we joining him?"

"For the last six months we've tried to find Woody in the hope of making a fortune," Fergal said. "Now that we've found him we ought to stay with him at least until we find out if he can make us as much money as he claims he can."

"Perhaps he can, but to me Woody seems a bit, well, sinister." Randolph pointed at their casket, now disappearing from sight. "For some reason when I helped him load that casket onto his wagon it was heavier than it was before."

"I don't view that as sinister. The only thing that interests me is that Woody reckons he knows how to use that casket to earn us a fortune. I reckon we should let him."

Randolph nodded reluctantly and moved over to take the reins, but before they could leave town Harlan emerged from the law office and he was scowling.

"Is Marshal Buckley all right?" Randolph asked.

"He's got a bust rib and plenty of bruises. The doctor says he'll be fine but everything else is wrong. That really was the last ever Marshal Blood adventure."

"He's still determined to resign?"

"Yeah." Harlan scowled. "He's decided to become a pig farmer, looking after Christopher Tate's pigs."

"Sounds like a good idea." Randolph offered Harlan a smile, which he didn't return. "He appeared to care more about pigs than the law."

"But the great Marshal Blood retiring to become a pig farmer isn't a suitable ending for my hero's last adventure."

"Then I guess you'll just need to find a different ending and a different hero."

Harlan kicked at the dirt, shaking his head, but then he stopped and looked up at Randolph, perhaps with a hint of adoration in his eyes. Then he roved his gaze on to Fergal. Slowly a smile appeared.

"Agreed," he said, brightening. "Perhaps I do know how to end my story, after all."

Randolph was about to ask for more details but Fergal leaned over to him.

"Come on, Randolph," he urged, "it's time to leave. There are plenty of fools out there with too much money in their pockets and too little sense in their heads who are just waiting for Woody's casket to come along and take it off them."

Randolph nodded and so with a last cheery wave to Harlan he shook the reins.

And so the two brave tonic sellers Fergal O'Brien and Randolph McDougal trundled their wagon out of town.

"Where shall we go now, Fergal?"

Fergal raised his chin as he looked ahead, his clear, honest eyes appraising the lowering sun.

"Somewhere out there, Randolph, there will be someone in need who we can help."

Randolph nodded. "And now that we know your tonic to cure all ills will not only help men but animals too, there are endless possibilities for the good we can do."

"That is so true." Fergal stood on the seat

and held a clenched hand to his chest. "Wher-
ever there's a wrong needing righted, my friend,
we have to be there."

Randolph agreed with this sentiment and so
with a whoop of bravura he shook the reins and
headed the horses off, directing their wagon towards the deep red sunset ahead in search of
more adventure.